USA TODAY BESTSELLING AUTHOR

Dale Mayer

I0587396

HEROES FOR HIRE

LIAM'S LILY: HEROES FOR HIRE, BOOK 15
Beverly Dale Mayer
Valley Publishing Ltd.

Copyright © 2018

ISBN-13: 978-1-773360-71-3
Print Edition

Books in This Series:

Carson's Choice: Heroes for Hire, Book 28
Dante's Decision: Heroes for Hire, Book 29
Steven's Solace: Heroes for Hire, Book 30

Boxed Sets and Bundles
https://geni.us/Bundlepage

About This Book

When former Navy SEAL Liam O'Brian joins Legendary Securities, he looks forward to being shipped somewhere exciting for his first mission with Levi and his crew. Instead, he learns exotic and enormous aren't exactly synonymous when he stumbles upon the oversized pachyderms inhabiting his new backyard. Still, conflicts are universal and Liam's troubles are only just beginning once he finds himself falling for a woman deeply rooted in her family's livelihood and problems.

Go-getter Lilianna Howell is a biologist who believes all problems can be reduced to minor ones if only they're nipped in the bud early enough. When her dad can no longer deal with the loss of his son and his detachment threatens the elephant reserve, Lilianna steps into a much larger role, handling the marketing and fundraising. Being close to her sister and her husband—once Lilianna's fiancé—forces her to struggle with distrust from that past experience and a growing attachment to a man who appears in her life like a dream come true.

Mammoth issues escalate as Liam and Lilianna team up to save the gentle giants, their newfound love… and their own lives.

Prologue

L IAM O'BRIEN PEERED out the garage window, watching as Brandon parked nearby. Rory and Michael stood at Liam's side as they watched their friend Brandon arrive with Kasha. They'd heard from Ice how crazy things got while saving Bullard and how it had ended up with another of their own finding a partner.

"Told you, Liam. Our unit is all here," Michael said quietly.

"And, except for you, Liam—and North—we're all taken," Rory added to Michael's comment.

"And it's a good thing too," Michael said. "We were all lost long enough. I never thought to find anyone who'd accept me or put up with me. But it's all good." He slapped Liam on the shoulder.

"I'm not sure I'm ready for this," Liam admitted. "It's one thing to be a part of this family connection you guys have going on, but it's a completely different issue to be standing on the outside and looking in. I'm not sure there's a place for me here. And, even if there is, I have no idea how to fit in."

"That's the thing. None of us did before we arrived. You have to trust you'll find your way."

Just then Brandon got out of the truck and stretched.

Damn, he looked good. Liam had been close to him—

Rory and Michael too—but there'd always been an extra connection between Liam and Brandon. And to see his buddy looking so happy, ... so fit—both emotionally and physically—well, it was a joy.

Liam would love and accept Kasha for that alone. They'd all had a hell of a last year with Levi and Ice establishing their new business—each member hiring on and finding their own perfect partner. Or almost everyone. Liam and North were both unattached. Then they were brand new to the team.

Brandon and Kasha, the happy couple, laughed and talked as they moved toward the kitchen door. Liam could hear their conversation.

"It's a good thing we took a week off before coming here." Kasha beamed at Brandon.

He chuckled. "In truth that week was like a mini-honeymoon."

Liam grinned at the flags of color blooming on Kasha's cheeks, but she didn't hide them. Instead she nodded. "It was indeed. It was also nice to see my family."

The huge double garage doors opened then. Liam glanced at Levi, who was manning the controls. Levi waited for the doors to lift fully, then stepped out.

"So much for being here when I arrived." Liam grinned at the blank look on Brandon's face before it lit up in joy.

The two men hugged each other.

Brandon stepped back to study Liam's face. "When the hell did you get here? You said you were considering it, not that you'd made up your mind." He slugged Liam on his shoulder. "Damn, it's good to see you."

"You haven't missed me at all," Liam scoffed, nodding to the stunning woman at Brandon's side.

"This is Kasha." Brandon held out his arm for her. She stepped close enough that his arm slid around her shoulder. "Kasha, this is my good friend Liam. He and I were in the same unit in the navy."

The smile Kasha flashed his way was both delightful and compassionate. Enough for Liam to know Brandon obviously cared a lot about this woman, especially if he'd shared some of these last few years' events.

Liam shook her hand. "Nice to meet you." He'd heard plenty about Kasha and Bullard and the nightmare Levi's team had gone through as they'd flown over to help out in Africa. "Too bad I didn't meet you first," he said in a teasing tone.

"There's a reason I overwhelmed her with my charms so fast." Brandon laughed. "You have a reputation with women …"

Kasha laughed. Liam gave her a lopsided grin, and her eyes widened. "Wow, that's a lethal smile."

Brandon tugged her close. "See?" he complained. "Women drop at his feet."

She sent Brandon a sideways glance. "I'm still standing."

He leaned over and kissed her. Then they both broke out laughing.

Just then Levi and Ice walked over. Ice smiled and said, "About time you two got here. We've got a crapload of work to do."

More of the clan arrived to greet the newcomers. Liam still struggled to remember everyone's name, and he'd been here a week already.

But Kasha walked in confidently, shaking hands with those she didn't know yet as she introduced herself.

"A lot of new faces around here," Levi said to Liam.

"It'll take me time to learn everybody's name," Liam replied.

Levi finished the introductions. He turned to both Brandon and Rory and asked, "You guys up for work? We weren't kidding about the jobs. We've caught several hot ones this morning alone."

Both men nodded, their faces brightening with interest. "We are so ready."

Levi turned to Kasha. "Are you on field duty or office work?"

She snorted. "Am I dead yet?"

Ice laughed. "That's my girl."

Levi gave her a wide smile and said, "Welcome. And goodbye. All three of you are leaving in the morning."

Liam looked from one to the other with a big smile. "What about me? Do you have something for me?" He'd done one short security job for Levi since he'd arrived, but, other than that, Liam had been setting up the new security-alarm-system side of the business. That had been fun, as he'd gotten to know several of the locals and had enjoyed being around the animals at Anna and Flynn's place. The puppies at the compound were adorable too. He was afraid to care and get his heart broken when they were adopted out—if they were adopted out. Something he knew Alfred and Bailey were fighting pretty hard against.

Levi chuckled. "If you want to go out on this one, you've got it."

Liam nodded. "I'm in."

"Be ready to leave by six a.m."

A collective groan ensued but not from Liam. He was energized. "That's awesome. Where are we going? Somewhere exotic, like Thailand? Maybe a sandy paradise, like the

Sahara? How about foggy Scotland?"

Ice, standing in the doorway, called out, "How about a big-animal reserve in Texas?"

He turned to her. "But we're in Texas now. There's nothing exotic about that."

She grinned. "Just you wait. Something very exotic is ahead for you."

On that cryptic note, she walked back inside, leaving Liam staring at her. He wasn't sure what she meant by that.

Levi smacked him on the shoulder. "Don't worry about it. Ice is good at this sort of stuff."

Liam looked at him suspiciously. "What sort of stuff?"

Levi had already stepped inside the house. He tossed back, "You'll find out soon enough. Just keep an open mind—and heart—and you'll be good."

At the open-heart comment, the others grinned, then laughed.

Liam stared at them. "What the hell did he mean by that?"

Everyone walked away, some laughing, others whistling.

Liam glared at Brandon, waiting for clarification.

Brandon shrugged. "Trust me. Like Levi said, you'll find out soon enough." Then Brandon walked inside with Kasha, leaving Liam alone to contemplate what everyone else already knew and what he had yet to find out.

Chapter 1

"OUR FIRST JOB together, working with Levi, that is. Interesting how that worked out." Liam turned to look at North sitting beside him, as Liam drove the double-cab pickup to their assignment. "Brandon, Rory, Kasha and I were supposed to be on this one, then another job came in, and they were reassigned."

"It happens." North chuckled. "Luckily, even with our delayed start, we'll still make it to meet the client on time. I highly suspect this job is a test," he said. "They figure, if we can handle this, we can handle anything."

"But really? An elephant sanctuary?" Liam asked. "I know I said I wanted to go to exotic places, but I wasn't thinking exotic animals in common places."

North laughed. "Honestly I'm delighted about spending some time in Texas. But this whole elephant thing? Well, that's a different story, although it is kind of exciting."

"Right? I wonder what kind of trouble they're having."

"You can bet, if it's a sanctuary, chances are it's probably a charity job. Levi and Ice are known for doing pro bono work."

"So they send the two new guys."

"Exactly. Still, the details are a little sketchy." North added, "I know we're supposed to see a Lilianna Howell."

Liam filed the name away in the back of his mind. "And

what has she got to do with this?"

"She's a biologist on staff at the sanctuary started by her father."

"Why elephants?"

"I guess they have the land for them. And that's a major part of what's required for elephants. Lots of space."

"I can see that," Liam said. "When you think about it, if a dog needs a certain amount, then a horse needs a proportionally larger amount, and an elephant? Wow, they've got to need hundreds of acres."

"I believe they have several square miles."

Liam took his glance off the road in front of him and shot North a look. "Seriously?"

North nodded and tapped the page in front of him. "Apparently."

"Well, that explains why we're in the middle of nowhere," Liam said. "And will be spending the next few days deeper in nowhere."

"Levi didn't say much about what the problem is," North said, flipping through the file.

"What he said just before he left was they suspect sabotage," Liam explained.

"Sabotage? I thought he said something about donations dwindling."

"Somebody was blackening their name to stop them from receiving charity donations, right?" Liam guessed.

"Ultimately Lilianna's afraid somebody's trying to shut them down," North said.

"Why would somebody care if she has a half-dozen elephants?"

"You and I both know it's never that simple."

"And since when are we investigating issues like that?"

Liam asked. "You know how many interesting cases have crossed Levi's desk?"

"I do." North laughed. "I've been hearing about them for a while."

Liam groaned. "Of course you have. I was thinking, you know, how we could go to Africa, maybe England, do something fun."

"I'm kind of thrilled about the elephants," North said.

Liam thought about that for a long moment. "I don't think I've ever been close to one."

"Neither have I. That's why I'm thrilled." North pointed at the sign up ahead. "End of Days Rest Home." He laughed. "That's got to be a joke."

"I doubt it. When you think an elephant can live longer than humans, that's a hell of a name. How far did the sign say the ranch is?"

"Seven miles."

Liam settled in for another few minutes' drive. The traffic was almost nonexistent. "Any coffee left?"

North nodded. "Alfred set us up with enough coffee for the two-hour drive. He wanted to send us off with a basket full of all kinds of goodies." North laughed. "I talked him out of that. But he was worried about us eating, since no *Alfred* exists where we were going and how pizza probably isn't delivered out here." North lifted the cloth insulated bag from the back seat to his lap, unzipped it, pulled out one of the two thermoses and refilled Liam's travel mug.

Liam murmured, "Thanks," and sipped his coffee with a pleased nod as he drove the truck just over the speed limit. When he saw the second sign up ahead, he slowed. "Looks like we're almost there."

Sure enough, another couple miles down the road he saw

the turnoff. He slowed even more, put on a signal, took the corner and headed toward what looked to be an official tourist building with a massive barn to one side and a huge residence on the other side. He pulled up out front of the business and sat inside the truck, staring at the size of the barn. "Will you look at that?"

"Like I said, proportionately, elephants will need a lot more space."

They hopped out and shut the truck doors. The barn rose high and wide. The fences were massive. Not just simple timber but appeared to be four-by-fours clamped together. Even at that, Liam imagined steel girders were inside for strength and the wood was more for a visual effect.

"What does it take to stop an elephant from going where the elephant wants to go?" Liam wondered aloud.

"There's not really anything man can do to stop an elephant who wants to go in a certain direction," a woman behind him said in a light and melodious voice.

He turned to see a woman with jet-black hair in a long braid down her back—tall, slim, dressed in jeans, a T-shirt and cowboy boots. He smiled, reached out a hand and said, "Liam O'Brien at your service."

She nodded to Liam and then turned, her eyebrows rising slightly at Liam's companion.

North stepped up and introduced himself.

She looked at them both and said, "Levi sent you?"

Just enough anxiousness was in her voice for them to immediately nod yes.

Relief washed over her face. "Well, thank heavens for that. He said he'd send someone, but ..." She shrugged.

"If Levi says he will, then he will," Liam said quietly. "I hear you've got yourself a spot of trouble."

"I just don't know how *big* a spot of trouble," she said with a nod. "It could be nothing. Maybe it's my imagination." She stared off in the direction where the highway went past her place. "It's just so hard to understand."

"If you'll fill us in, we'll do what we can to help you get to the bottom of it," Liam said with a smile.

North motioned toward the office and said, "Shall we go in?"

Her face cleared. "Oh, my goodness, yes. Of course. I'm so sorry for making you stand out here."

Liam shrugged. "It can be here or there. It doesn't matter. But the sooner we understand what's happening, the sooner we can help you."

She nodded and ushered them toward the door.

Liam didn't know if it was the way she always moved, but her long legs ate up the distance quickly. Inside she didn't slow down. She kept on toward the back of the building. He vaguely saw a reception area and what looked like a tourist section with information on elephants in the bookcases against the wall. "Do you do public tours here?"

She nodded. "We do some. Mostly schools and educational trips. We've got a lot of seniors who come out once a week."

That surprised him. This place was a long way from anywhere. But, of course, it was only an hour from the closest city. Or rather the outskirts of Houston. Levi's compound was on the other side of Houston, about an hour away. So that made their one-way trip at least two hours long.

Inside a small room, she motioned at two chairs, then walked around behind the desk. "Please have a seat." She reached behind her and pulled out a large file. She flipped it over on the desk so they could reach it. "This is what I have.

I've sent most of it to Levi."

Liam picked up the folder, and, with North looking on, Liam opened it up and flipped through the various pamphlets. There was a bunch of printed screenshots. "What is it you're disturbed about here?" He tried not to look as confused as he felt. "I see a lot of screenshots from a website."

She nodded. "Yes, various pages are showing up when they shouldn't be," she said. "I'm confused myself. But a lot of people have said they have tried to make donations, and, when they go through the payment process, a warning sign comes up, saying the place has been known to be a scam and to send the money elsewhere."

"It directly called you a scam and redirected people to donate elsewhere?" North asked. He shook his head. "That makes no sense."

"Right? That's what I told my sister," Lilianna said. "I think we are being targeted because there's no other reason to deliberately stop donations from coming in. It doesn't say it's a security alert to get people to walk away, but it's a deliberate *this site is a charity scam.*"

"Any idea how much money you may have lost?"

She shook her head. "It's hard to know," she admitted. "Normally I would have anywhere between $6,000 and $8,000 brought in at this time of the month. We're at less than $1,000."

Liam stared at her. "You get that kind of donations?"

She nodded. "And we need them. Keeping the animals, vet bills, feed …" She shook her head again. "It's very expensive."

He stared out the window. "I guess my first thought would be, maybe a disgruntled employee?"

She sagged back. "That's what I thought too, but we don't really have any."

He wondered at the truth of that. Whether she knew it or not, very few people were ever 100 percent satisfied with their jobs.

"How many people do you employ?"

"Four permanent employees right now, several more on contract, like the vet, and of course I have secondary workers also on contract—a bookkeeper, tax man, stuff like that. Plus a webmaster and people who do marketing for us."

"Well, the webmaster would be the first place to start," North declared. "Do you have contact information for him?"

She nodded, dug through an old-fashioned Rolodex card file on the side of her desk while they watched in astonishment. She glanced up as she pulled out the card. "I know, right? But I haven't had time to make my system digital yet," she confessed. "This is my father's old system. He never trusted technology."

Liam smiled. "That's not unusual." He was relieved to see an email address, phone number and a physical address were all on the card. "Can you copy this for us?" He glanced around. "Do you have a printer?"

"I do. I insisted on one for the business. But my father didn't like it." She chuckled, turned around to uncover the copier, copied the card, handed it to him and then refiled the card where it belonged in the Rolodex.

He took the sheet and added it to the file. "We'll begin with him. What else do we have as options?"

They went through the file folder, and, although it was thick, it seemed to be more like a marketing package.

Just then an alarm rang.

Lilianna bounced to her feet. "I've got to run." She raced

out of the building through a back door. Liam was up and after her in a heartbeat. He knew North was following, presumably with the folder in his hand, but Liam didn't stop to look. He raced behind her, catching up to her with some effort as she could clip along at quite the pace.

"What is that alarm for?"

"We're having trouble with one of the elephants," she said, "and that's the handler calling out a distress signal."

She bolted into the barn through the large doors, and he stopped. These were no normal stalls. They were made of four-inch pipe aligned into what would have been the equivalent of a horse barn stall. The ceiling was at least twenty feet high above him, if not thirty feet. The barn was more open than usual with walkways through the center, but the pens for the animals were huge, and each one had a rear door leading outside.

In one pen he could see an elephant, but the noise it made caught him by surprise. The trumpeting. The elephant had its trunk held up, and it was crying out.

A man looked up as Lilianna walked in. "There you are," he said with relief. He looked at the elephant's foot. "We need the vet here. She's got something in her foot."

Lilianna let herself into the pen, walked over as she gently talked to the animal. "Let me take a look. Take it easy, Billie. You'll be just fine."

But Billie wasn't having anything to do with it.

Finally Lilianna got the elephant to calm down enough that she could check the foot. Liam had been around enough horses to know how to lift a hoof to check for rocks in the shoes, but he'd never, ever seen the size of a foot like this elephant had. Lilianna knelt, taking a close look, and between her and the handler, they managed to pull out something that was stuck.

With that removed, they cleaned out the wound, and Lilianna stepped back. The elephant nudged her big head, plowing into Lilianna's chest gently. Lilianna wrapped her arms around the trunk and laid her head against the huge animal's face and said, "It's okay. It's not that big of an *owie*."

With an odd chuffing sound, the trunk wrapped around her.

Liam stared.

North, standing beside him, said, "Just a big overgrown puppy."

Liam shook his head. "Good Lord."

With her arms wrapped around Billie, Lilianna took her out the stall's rear door, and, as if knowing now she would be okay, Billie walked into the sunshine, with no sign of a limp. Lilianna stood there for a long moment, checking her gait; then she came back over and said, "Thanks, Daniel, for giving me a call."

"You know? I keep thinking I can handle these guys. But honestly they're so attached to you, they don't really like anybody else working on them," Daniel said. "As soon as I realized she was injured, she caterwauled like a baby and wouldn't let me even touch her foot."

Lilianna chuckled. "She *is* a big baby."

Daniel nodded. "She is the worst for that. I can get almost any of the others to cooperate. But Billie wants you."

"Billie is also the oldest here," she explained to Liam. "She'll be twenty-one this year."

Liam looked at her. "That's an old age for any pet."

She laughed. "Elephants are notoriously long lived."

"Her foot seemed to be healthy though," North said.

"Outside of whatever it was you pulled out."

"It was a big piece of glass," she said, anger in her voice. "And I have no idea where she picked it up." She turned to Daniel. "Was she just in the yard?"

He nodded. "Yes. And you know we've gone over that yard with rakes a dozen times. I don't know where she got it from."

Lilianna walked to where she'd placed the offending piece and picked it up, taking it to the men. "This is the third piece we've picked up. I found one in the yard. One of the dogs got cut on another one."

"Where did you find the one in the yard?" North asked.

She motioned toward the entranceway. "It was right at the front entrance, where it was pretty hard for anybody to miss."

"Do you think it was done deliberately?" Liam asked. He glanced at the four-inch piece of glass. "That's a hell of a weapon."

"I know," she snapped. "And it pisses me right off."

"How many people have access to this area?"

Daniel spoke up, answering, "Just those of us who work here. That's the problem. It's like somebody's deliberately making it look like it's one of us." He shook his head. "I've spent ten years here. I'd never do anything to hurt them."

"After ten years, Billie still won't let you touch her feet?"

Daniel laughed. "Exactly. She is Lilianna's baby."

Lilianna grinned. "I have to admit, she does have her fancies. But she's a good-hearted girl. She'd never hurt a soul."

"Where are you getting all these elephants from?"

She sighed and brushed a few loose tendrils of hair off her forehead. "Anywhere, really," she said quietly. "A couple are from circuses. A couple are from zoos. We had one come down from Canada. It's a long journey for these animals. It can easily take a week to truck them. But it's the only way to get them to us. Here they get to live out the rest of their lives in peace and quiet."

Liam was stunned. He'd heard about places like this, but he had never thought to be in one. "Do you think whoever is doing this actively hates that you're helping elephants? Or do you think it's a personal affront against you or perhaps your father?"

The other three looked at him in surprise. Daniel was most stunned. "Well, that's a horrible suggestion."

Liam gave him a bland look. "If somebody's doing something to destroy the name of the sanctuary, the end result is the animals will suffer. So you have to consider that maybe it's done for that reason alone. The other option is that it's done to ruin the good name of the people involved."

Lilianna took a few steps until she was out of the pen. She motioned at Daniel. "Are you done here? Or will you stay with Billie a little longer to ensure she's all right?"

"I'll clean up here for a bit," he said. "I'll keep looking for more glass, check on Billie."

Lilianna led the way back through the stalls. "I can't imagine any reason why somebody would do this, but then I don't understand that mind-set anyway," she said quietly.

"Right," Liam said. "So we have to consider all options." He stopped and looked around the barn. "How often do you get a new elephant in?"

"Not very often. The logistics to bring them here are a nightmare."

"I remember hearing something in the news about trucking three elephants down from Canada. The cost was like a half-million dollars, although I believe those three went to California."

"I know. It shouldn't be that expensive. But, by the time you add in the trucking fees, the couple dozen men required and all the transportation costs, it comes to something like that. I believe that was for two elephants though."

Liam shook his head. "And all the money was donated in that case?"

"Yes. Gunner donated to the cause. A television personality put the charity event together to make it happen. They get a little more publicity because they're a little more well-known, but still any organization who needs donations to keep functioning has to continually publicize. That's why we do the schools. But some of the animals don't do all that well with people. Even though two of ours were circus animals, it's like, once they managed to get away from people, they didn't really want anything to do with humans again."

"And Billie?"

She chuckled. "Billie? …Well, she's a people person. It's not that she loves to perform, but she's like a big puppy dog. She loves attention."

"So you let people touch her, things like that?" North asked.

She nodded. "Absolutely. Mandy is here too, and she's very similar. She and Billie are best friends."

"Is it true they remember each other if they haven't seen each other in a long time?"

"Mandy and Billie were from the same herd out of Africa, and, when they saw each other again for the first time here, they recognized each other immediately and were inseparable. The first thing they did when they got close enough was wrap their trunks around each other. We had to separate them in order to get them out of the transport. Once they were outside, they wrapped their trunks around each other and just stood together. Honestly it was incredibly heartwarming and brought tears to my eyes."

"And where would Mandy be now?"

Lilianna pointed toward the yard, the other side of the door Billie had walked out of. "She'll be out there."

"How much space do they have access to here?"

"A lot," she admitted. "Almost two thousand acres. And they do travel at various times. But they always like to come back home again. The other three stay together a little farther away from the barn. They come back on a regular basis. We check them over, make sure we can still handle them, but, unlike Mandy and Billie, they're enjoying retirement. And, of course, that means something different to everyone. In their case, they just want time out in Mother Nature without any interference."

"It's an amazing concept you have here," North said. "Do you have other animals?"

She nodded. "We do. We have some horses, which makes it easier for us to check up on the elephants. We have two goats that are always with the three elephants, and of course we have dogs."

"But you're a sanctuary only for elephants?" Liam asked.

She nodded. "For the moment, yes. I'd like to expand our concept to accept other big animals. But it'll take a hell of a lot more money than I have right now to do that."

LILIANNA STARED AT the two newcomers. She chewed on her bottom lip, wondering how much she should tell them. She'd seen their assessing gazes and realized they were no slouches. But then what would she expect? Logan had recommended Levi. And Logan's father, Gunner, had contacted Levi on her behalf. She didn't know what she would do without Gunner. His donations went a long way to keeping these elephants in great shape. She wanted to expand to assisting more animals. But it required a certain expertise and more money for pens and housing. Not to mention ongoing funds for food and medical attention. And yet she was driven to do this. She wasn't here on the land as much as she should be as she was constantly traveling to drum up funds.

Her sister Brianna was here most of the time. Since they were identical twins, it was easy to get them confused. Her sister had often stepped into her place, not necessarily in a good way. And of course Lilianna's mind immediately went down the rabbit hole to her ex-fiancé who was now her sister's husband. Her sister was devoted to this place, but Lilianna wasn't sure that her husband, Carlos, was devoted to anything but himself.

It had taken her too long to understand, and it had taken even longer to realize what he was up to. By then her sister was fully hooked and even more so because Carlos had been Lilianna's first. She turned to the two men. "I don't know what you need to figure out what's going on," she said, "but you should understand there are a few other players here."

Liam faced her, nodding slowly. "I would suspect there are," he said with a drawl.

Something about his accent sent shivers down her spine. She forced a bigger smile and said, "There are some hard feelings around here, but nothing that isn't normal within a family."

"And what family would that be?" North asked.

Just then a bang came from the house on the other side. The men turned at the noise to watch another woman striding toward them. Instead of watching her sister arrive, Lilianna focused on Liam's face, caught the surprise as he narrowed his gaze in assessment. It was an interesting look. She wondered what was going through his mind.

Brianna arrived just then and glared at the men. "Who the hell are you?"

Lilianna sighed. "This is my twin sister, Brianna."

The men nodded, and Liam offered an explanation. "We're here to investigate the problems in the sanctuary."

Brianna sniffed, raised her nose in the air and said, "Then you can get the hell off the place because nothing's going on here. My sister is just a worrywart. She has no clue how to run this place."

Lilianna rubbed her temple. If there was one thing she would like her twin to do, it would be to stop belittling her in front of everyone. But it had always been that way. Brianna was the bigger, more outgoing, bossier type of person. Lilianna was reserved, one of the doers of the world. She always did the work behind the scenes so other people could step up and take the spotlight from her. She didn't mind. She was a worker. She'd rather be with the animals than dealing with people anyway. But, at the same time, this wasn't the time or place for sibling crap.

"Brianna, we talked about this," Lilianna said. "You know perfectly well we are having trouble."

"So what? You bring in these two?" She waved her hand carelessly at the two men. "For what?"

It was hard not to miss the two men's stiffened backs, as if dismissed as some useless laborers.

Brianna snorted and stormed toward the barn. "They'll just screw up everything. I told you, you shouldn't come back. Everything is fine." And her sister slammed the door going into the barn.

In the distance Lilianna heard an elephant trumpet. She shoved her fists into her pockets and sighed. "As you can tell, there's a little bit of disagreement."

The two men stared in the direction Brianna had gone.

"How does a reaction like that affect the elephants?" Liam asked.

Startled at the question, she shrugged. "Like any household, strife ripples outward. The elephants are much better away from all of it. However, Brianna does share in their care, depending on Daniel's schedule. I would normally, but she wanted to handle the business side and to stay here all the time, so I'm now doing the fund-raising and need to travel a lot."

"You're the one who knows Gunner?"

She nodded. "And Logan."

The men smiled.

She grinned at them. "And, yes, I can see you guys are the same as he is. The thing is? My sister doesn't have any use for Logan either." She gave a half grin. "He turned her down. She doesn't take rejection easily."

A curious light came into Liam's gaze as he studied her. "And you? Do you take rejection easily?"

She laughed a real laugh. "I'm used to it. I take rejection just fine," she said, her voice dry. "But then I'm always the one in the background. I don't expect very much. So, when I get rejected, it's just the norm." With the men staring at her as if waiting for an explanation, she raised both hands in mock surrender and said, "I'm always the worker. I'm not the face on the brochures. Even though you probably look at them and see me, it's her. Some history is in there. We also had an older brother, but he passed away a couple years back in a fire." She had a sad smile now. "And I think Brianna felt like she had to step in to take care of what would normally have been his role."

"Was he as passionate about this job as your father?"

She nodded. "He was indeed. I am too. I love to be around the animals. But the family situation isn't the best, and I'd rather not leave my sister here to run this. I'm here as much as I can be though." She ended that on a laugh. "Other than that, I'm always traveling around, trying to drum up money."

"That can't be easy."

She shook her head. "No, it's not. I'm also the one who updates the website."

"Not the webmaster?" North asked, his tone hard.

She shook her head. "No, the webmaster is there if I need help. But you got to pay them by the hour, so I do as much as I can by myself."

"And let me guess? Your sister blames you because of the website issues?"

She winced. "How did you know?"

Liam didn't say anything as his gaze searched the surrounding area. "Are there any other houses on the property?"

"I have a small cabin in the back," Lilianna said. "My sister has the family home with her husband."

They studied her carefully.

She shrugged. "It's not like I can turn around and build a second house on the sanctuary."

"Would you want to?"

"If I were to do that, I'd bring my father back out here,"

she said softly.

"Where is your father now?"

"In town." She refused to elaborate. There was only so much personal stuff she wanted to deal with in the first thirty minutes of meeting these men.

"What does the husband do?"

"Carlos? He's some kind of an investment advisor," she said airily, waving her hand toward the house. "I'm not exactly sure."

"How long have they been married?"

"About eighteen months." She stared at the house. "But they've been together for a couple years."

"Interesting."

She spun and looked at Liam with a sharp gaze, but neither man said anything else. "I did promise Levi that I had a place to put you up, but it's not fancy."

The men stared at her blandly.

"Originally I thought you could stay in the big house, but Brianna said no."

"I hope you have a little more than a hay loft," Liam said with a grin. "It's not that I'm against sleeping with the animals. But ..."

"It depends whether you're okay to stay with me or not," she said abruptly. She studied the two of them. "Levi said I could trust you, which is the only reason I make that offer ..." Her voice trailed off as she realized for the first time that a problem could arise from something completely different than feeling unsafe.

These men looked like protectors, like guardians. They were cut from the same cloth as Logan. They were men, as in *real* men, in all senses of the word. What she hadn't expected was to feel her heart tug every time she looked at Liam. The last thing she wanted was to have her heart in danger. That wasn't what they were here for; it wasn't what she wanted them for.

But she wasn't sure she would have a choice about this.

Chapter 2

S HE WATCHED AS Liam's eyebrows rose.

"Is the cabin big enough?" he asked cautiously.

"There's a loft with two beds in it."

"Then it's big enough," North said carelessly.

"We're easy to please. As long as you have food," Liam said, his gaze twinkling.

It had been a long time since she'd seen that level of humor and the mischievous teasing-little-boy look in his eyes. It was hard not to respond to Liam. She gave him a big wink and said, "There's food. But you might have to cook it yourself."

Both men's faces fell.

She laughed. "I can cook, but it's pretty simple fare. If you're expecting fancy, that won't happen."

The men shook their heads. "We're fine with plain fare," Liam assured her. "If you'll take us to the cabin first, so we can unpack, then we'll head out for a walk around to get the lay of the land."

"I have to come with you," she said. "It's the only way I could get Brianna to agree."

"You think we'll steal an elephant?" North asked in astonishment.

"No. I *think* Brianna just wants to make sure we're not held responsible for any of the sabotage that's occurred."

"Yet she just said nothing was going on here. You definitely need to tell us what's been happening here. So let's get to the cabin. Maybe you've got coffee?" Liam asked hopefully. "We'll need to take some notes. Levi had very little information for us."

Lilianna nodded. "I know. I didn't give him a whole lot. Gunner knows more of the story."

"How long have you known Gunner?" North asked as they returned to the truck.

"Years," she said with a smile. "Logan and I were friends way back when too."

"Did you date?"

Surprised at the personal level of the question, she turned to study Liam's face. But only an honest curiosity was there. She shook her head. "No. He was my brother's friend first. I was the kid sister who hung around," she said with a laugh. "Logan was fun to be around. He's always been supersupportive of our sanctuary."

"It's not like most people get to see an elephant every day," Liam said. "I'll have to contact Logan to get his take on things."

"I think Gunner deliberately didn't tell you very much so you would get your own impressions," she said, frowning.

"Of course," Liam said. "But Logan's one of us. And to have insider knowledge like he has would give us a leg up."

She shrugged. "Whatever." She pointed at their truck. "Bring the truck up and around the back." She pointed to the driveway that curved ahead of them. "I'll open the gate for you."

At that point they split up. The men headed to the truck, and she walked back around the property to the gate.

The storefront and offices had been the original homestead house. But once they started the sanctuary, they needed a tourist center. And that was what the existing house became. Her father had built a new one to make the transition. She and her sister had grown up there. Along with Keith. Now that he was gone, things had changed. Not the least of which was her father. He'd had trouble dealing with Keith's death.

Lilianna opened the gate, pulling it wide as they drove up and around the office. She waited until they passed, then closed the gate, making sure it clicked into place. She walked toward the truck.

As she approached, the door opened on the passenger side, and North got out. "Do you want a lift?"

She leaned through the driver's window, pointed to the tracks heading over the rise. "We're going up there. I'll sit in the bed." She walked to the back of the truck, hopped up into the bed and sat on one of the fender wells.

Liam drove forward at a reasonably slow pace. Up over the rise she could see her place. The window between the cab and the bed was open to allow for fresh air. She leaned forward. "That's the cabin over there."

Liam nodded obediently and turned the truck in that direction. He pulled up in front of her small place. She jumped out of the bed and waited for the men to join her. Moon Dog and Boomer came over to greet her. She introduced them to the men.

The men looked around, and Liam said, "The dogs and the elephants don't have a problem?"

"We do have a fence on the other side of that rise. I'll let the elephants in on this side every once in a while, but otherwise we keep them over there."

Liam nodded. "I imagine having them come up to the

kitchen window and stick a trunk in, looking for a treat, might be a bit unnerving."

She grinned. "The elephants were free to do that for the longest time. Before we got all the fences built, the elephants became family to us," she said. "And honestly they're not a bad family to have."

She led the way inside as both dogs checked out the two new arrivals. She stopped on the top step and watched as the men, instead of following her, bent to say hi to the dogs. She smiled. You could always tell what kind of men they were by the treatment of the animals around them. Her dogs were supposed to be guard dogs, but they had a tendency to love everyone regardless. Too bad they weren't a great judge of character as she could think of a couple lousy boyfriends they shouldn't have liked so well.

Inside she said, "As you can see, it's small, but it's all I need."

The two men stood in the middle of the living room and looked around. Given their size, they pretty well dwarfed the area.

She walked to the little kitchen and put on a pot of coffee. "My bedroom is at the back. You guys can take the loft."

The two men took the small staircase at the far corner, each carrying a bag.

She called up, "You might as well open the window and let some fresh air in."

She smiled to herself. The weather was all over the place right now. It was cold enough at times in the winter to light the fire. But, right now, it was spring, and she was more concerned about how fertile the land was and whether they'd end up with a dry burn area this year or if she'd have decent grass. Grass fires were still an ever-present danger. The elephants had a lot of range to roam, and that was good.

She was just pouring the coffee when the men came back down the stairs. It was obvious they'd been talking. She'd heard their voices but nothing specific. She pushed two cups across the small counter and said, "Coffee is ready."

"Thanks," Liam said.

"Do you live here alone?" North asked.

She shot him a look. "Are you asking if I have a boy-friend? Because that's a whole different story."

"No," he said easily. "That's not what I'm asking."

"I live alone."

The men both nodded.

She picked up her mug of coffee and walked to the couch. "You realize there's nothing terribly dangerous about this job, right? I'm not being threatened. There have been no attacks on humans. Nothing like that." She wasn't sure what they'd been told.

Both men again nodded.

She sighed. "Feels really weird to have you here."

"We can stay in town if you want," Liam said. "We certainly don't want to make you feel uneasy."

She shook her head. "At least if you're here, you can see if anything happens on the premises."

"Things like what?"

"Tiny, minor things. Except that ..." Her voice rose with each word. "Sorry, I don't mean to snap."

The men just nodded.

She groaned. She really needed to tell them. "Before you find out through staff and whatever rumors might be circulating, Carlos and I were engaged. Then he transferred his affections to my sister," she said in a dry tone.

The men looked at her, their expressions schooled.

"Right? I know. We look the same so maybe that's not to be unexpected," she said, her words rushing into the empty space around her. "Whatever. I just wanted you to know."

"I'm sorry," Liam said.

His next words startled her.

"It's hard enough to deal with rejection, but, when the rejection is for a carbon copy of yourself, that must add further confusion to the whole thing."

"We're the same on the outside," she said. "But we're very different on the inside." She stared at her coffee cup. "Okay. Let's go through whatever it is you need to know."

"We need a list of all the staff members who work here and have worked here for the last ten years," North said.

"We also need contact information for all of them," Liam said. "We need access to your website from the back end, so we can take a look at the programming."

"Are you programmers?" she asked in hopeful delight.

"No, but we're techie enough. We promise we won't mess up your system. Also Levi does have access to some really good computer people. If we can't find anything, or we see something we can't deal with, we won't hesitate to bring on their team."

Lilianna nodded, feeling something settle inside. "That's very reassuring. I hate to say that something's going on, but obviously it is… It's extremely unnerving…"

"We also need a list of people who have publicly voiced their disapproval about the sanctuary, and those who have potentially tried to besmirch the family name, your father's work, the sanctuary itself, you and/or your sister."

She winced. "Do you have any idea how hard it'll be to pull that list together?"

"We do. But how else do you expect us to look at who and what might have done this if we don't have a direction to head in?"

Her shoulders sagged, and she curled up into her chair. The two men sat on the only couch in the living room. For just herself, the place was more than big enough. But these two men with such overly large presences made her feel diminutive and her cabin positively tiny. "I'll do what I can." She frowned. "What about contract workers, like accountants?"

They nodded. "Everyone," Liam emphasized. "Somebody is doing this. We need to find out who and why."

"We also need the dates of important events for the last ten years," North added.

At that, she stared at Liam first, then back at North, her jaw dropping. "What do you mean by *important events?*"

The two men exchanged hard glances and then both shot laser looks back at her. "Something triggered this," Liam said gently. "But that doesn't mean it was triggered recently. Sometimes people take weeks and months to work up to doing something they feel they have a right to do. So we want to know back ten years. When the first elephant and the next elephant arrived, where it came from, what kind of outcry there was at her arrival, the official cause of your brother's death, the problems with your father, when Carlos came into your life, when he switched to being in your sister's life, when they got married, etc."

She sat back and stared. "Will you leave any rock in my life unturned?" she snapped.

The men looked at her. Liam said, "Honestly? No."

33

LILIANNA REALLY HAD no idea just how much her wish for privacy wouldn't matter soon. The men did their best, but an investigation like this, where it was likely to be more about personal issues than business concerns, would be incredibly intrusive. Liam didn't know what was going on behind this, but there were a lot of players, and they had to figure it out fast.

That Gunner had sent her to Levi was also huge. It meant that Gunner, who already knew what Levi's talent base was and what kind of information they could ferret out, trusted their team. And also that he realized this was a big issue. He was pouring a lot of money into keeping these animals safe, so who would want to stop that? Someone who thought the money should go to a better place? Or who wanted it for themselves?

"How long has your family had the land?"

Lilianna looked at North in surprise. "It's been in the family for several generations."

"And how long have you had elephants here?"

"About fifteen years now," she said with a smile. "We brought the second one in to keep the first one company. And it just carried on from there."

"Do you have more coming in?"

She nodded. "We're trying to get two more."

"Any sign of that causing a problem?"

She shook her head. "No, but it takes time and a lot of paperwork, not to mention organization. Often the elephants have injuries, usually foot injuries, and can't stand still for too many hours at a time. They have to have special spots to be unloaded. You can't keep them locked up in a trailer for seven days," she joked. "The logistics can be quite challenging."

The men nodded. Liam looked around at the small cabin. "Who lived here before you?"

She raised her eyebrows. "It used to be staff housing."

"It feels like there should be more buildings, more staff housing."

She nodded. "Several cabins are on the other side. At one point, a lot of cattle were run on this property. Those cabins are not in the best of shape," she admitted.

"Money only goes so far, doesn't it?"

She laughed and nodded. "There's never enough."

"Have you always wanted to be here?"

She shook her head. "No. But you have to realize my mother left when I was eleven. Dad got his first elephant about that time too. He built the main house not too long afterward. It was all a big adjustment. And Brianna was … being Brianna even back then. I couldn't wait to leave for college and got my degree as a biologist. I was doing research. Yet I helped my dad and brother from the start, as much as a preteen girl could do with a four-ton elephant. In college, I helped my father and brother on the side, setting up the website and doing the advertising. I don't think either of them had any idea just how expensive it would be otherwise." She chuckled. "My father's stubborn, and so am I. Then I received several grants for more work on the elephants, so I got more involved with the sanctuary. But my focus really changed after Keith's death to looking after the sanctuary on a full-time basis."

"Has your father lived here all his life?"

"Yes." She stared at the newer house down the road. "He built the big house after my mother left, so about fifteen years ago roughly."

"No dispute over where you should live versus where

they should live?"

She shrugged.

Liam caught a glimpse of pain on her face. He couldn't help but wonder what kind of a relationship the twin sisters had left after the switch of a fiancé, who was now a husband. "Does Carlos live here on the place?"

She shook her head. "No, he likes to think he does. But he's rarely here, and he's more in the way than anything."

Her words was brusque, but there didn't appear to be any animosity in it. He tucked that information away for later. "Internet?"

She smiled. "Yes, I have internet."

"In that case," Liam said, "we'll grab our laptops and notepads so we can get started."

Liam rose and walked up the small flight of stairs to the loft. For a small cabin it was extremely well made. Like so many of the older things, they were built to last forever, not just for the moment. A bed was on either side of the loft. The loft itself wasn't terribly tall. He could walk through it in the center but had to duck to go to the sides. He pulled out his laptop, grabbed North's laptop sitting on his bed, and, noting power bars for each, he carried them downstairs, handing North his gear. Then Liam searched for a plug, smiled when he saw one not far away and brought up his laptop.

Lilianna said nervously, "Levi said he would help cover the costs of having you guys here."

North looked at her. "That was nice of him." His voice was neutral.

She winced. "It's more than nice," she admitted. "I feel really bad accepting more charity from them. It's bad enough you guys are here, and we can't pay your normal rates.

Gunner said he'd strike up a deal, but I know that it'll not be a whole lot of cash coming from my place."

"You did say you had food though, right?" Liam teased.

She chuckled. "Speaking of which, there might be a piece of cake left." She wandered into the small kitchen.

Liam couldn't take his eyes off her. She was tall and willowy with long hair in a single braid down her back. Her hair was almost black, her skin white, her eyes green, and it was such an odd thing to see together and to focus on. Having both of the twins here and looking so much the same, it was like twice the oddity. Yet Lilianna appealed to him. Her sister didn't. There was a harder edge to Brianna, whereas Lilianna had a fresh innocence to her. That country-girl look, wearing her cowboy boots like she'd been born and bred into them.

She opened a bread box on the counter and pulled out a container. He watched hopefully as she lifted the lid, and sure enough there was a slab of chocolate cake.

"Did you bake that?"

She nodded as she got them each a slice. "I did. Every once in a while, I get a sweet tooth, and I end up going crazy baking. It's not the best thing for me though."

He frowned. What was the problem? She was not only lean and slim but he couldn't see an ounce of fat on her.

"Why not?" North asked.

She glanced at him and smiled. "Blood sugar issues," she said. "I had a pancreatic attack when I was younger. Every once in a while, my blood sugar gives me some trouble. And, of course, sugar in the form of cakes and bread is definitely not the healthiest choices I could make."

"Did your sister also have a similar attack?"

"No. There are differences between us."

"It must have been fun growing up as part of a twin though."

"Sometimes, yes, but sometimes it felt like I was just a blander, paler, less vibrant copy of my sister."

Yet to Liam it was the opposite.

She brought the cake over and handed them each a plate and fork, picked up their cups and refilled them. "I meant it when I said I'm a plain cook." She glanced at the clock. "I plan to put on pasta for dinner around five, if that's okay with you guys."

That hint of nervousness in her voice made Liam wonder what was really going on. He nodded. "That's fine. We're easy to please." He could see the relief on her face and wondered about that. "How often do you see Gunner?"

Her face softened. "Gunner is a sweetheart. I try to stop in and see him every time I'm in town. I try to go more often than when I need money," she joked. "The last thing I want him to think is that I'm only there for that."

"Gunner is very generous," Liam said. "I know he helps Anna and her rescue center out a lot too."

"I haven't met her yet, but I have met Flynn many times," she said.

"Anna is a sweetheart too. She'll do anything for any animal or reptile," Liam said. "I'm surprised she hasn't visited here."

At that Lilianna's face brightened. "She is coming. Logan promised to bring them both in a couple weeks."

"Good," he said. "You'll love her. She's all heart."

She gave him an odd look. "Good, the world needs more people like that."

"When can we see your father?" North asked.

It was a good thing Liam was watching her and caught

the pain as it crossed her face.

"How about never?" she said drily.

The men looked at her and froze. "What are you talking about?" Liam asked.

"He hasn't been the same since my brother's death," she said sadly. "Even if you do see him, I'm not sure we can get him to talk."

Chapter 3

TWO HOURS LATER, Lilianna stood. She waved a shaky hand at the men. "That was exhausting," she said, handing over the lists the guys had asked for. "I'll begin dinner. You can talk to me while I cook."

"We have a list of names to check out, a list of dates here to work from." Liam stood, stretching as he walked around the small space. "Where can we set up something like a whiteboard or maybe use a wall to pin things for a time line?"

She glanced at him, her head tilted. "Upstairs in the loft? Nobody else will see it, if people come and go."

He considered that and nodded. "You know? That might work. I just need pins and some kind of paper or poster board."

She walked over to a drawer. When opened, he could see it held a hammer, screwdrivers and a bunch of odds and ends.

She pulled out a pack of straight pins. "Will this work?"

He nodded. "They will indeed." He glanced over at North. "What do you think?"

North stood. "While she cooks, I suggest we get a start on a time line."

The two men disappeared upstairs. She wasn't sure what advantage a time line would give them. As far as she was concerned, it had nothing to do with their current issues. But Gunner had put his faith into Levi and his crew, so she would do the same. She diced an onion while the ground meat cooked beside her. She hated this feeling of intense weariness.

She'd been thinking that she'd done a good job in dealing with all the family problems, but the more she talked about it, the more she realized she hadn't really dealt with it at all. Her brother's death. Her father's declining health. Her sister marrying Carlos. Still so much anger and maybe even fear remained inside her.

As she chopped, she thought about the consequences of her sister marrying her previous lover. And how uncomfortable it was to be around them even now. Her sister felt the same way. But then why not? They'd loved the same man. They were both prepared to marry the same man. In fact, her sister had gone ahead and done it. Lilianna would have too, if her dearly beloved fiancé hadn't decided to sleep with her sister weeks before they were to marry. And, if that wasn't a blow to her self-confidence, she didn't know what was.

To spend all that time supposedly in love with one sister and then to hop into bed with the other and decide that was who you wanted instead, how did that work? She shook her head, forcibly changing the direction of her thoughts.

With the onions in the pan, she brought out the garlic and had it minced within seconds. Food prep was good therapy. Next she chopped celery, then diced some fresh tomatoes. She put on a big pot full of salted water and got the pasta cooking. As she stood, she could hear the men above, their voices muted.

When her phone rang, she stared at it for a long moment, wondering if she was up to dealing with her sister.

Twins were supposed to be close. They were supposed to be best friends. But somehow, somewhere along the line, her sister and she had lost that connection. Instead it had been more like a competition until Lilianna had completely given up on the competition aspect and willingly stepped into her sister's shadow. Why had she done that? Inside, she knew it was for the sake of peace. Her sister had always been very confrontational. Ready to fight Lilianna, the softer, gentler sister, and blast her into oblivion if she didn't follow Brianna's orders.

And she'd let her. It had been so much easier. Her father had once mentioned it to her, and, when she explained what was going on, her father sighed and said, "That was my marriage. I was you, and your dearly beloved mother was Brianna."

The two had hugged, knowing they were both the softer souls in this world. It didn't mean Lilianna was weak though, and that was the mistake her sister always made. Brianna always took what she wanted, so, when it came to Lilianna's husband-to-be, she'd done the same thing. She had snatched up Carlos, completely wrapped him in her web, and that was it. It didn't matter that Lilianna had loved him. It didn't matter that they were engaged to be married. No, it was entirely all about what Brianna wanted.

At the same time, Lilianna worked hard to stop feeling sorry for herself. She wasn't a victim, and she would never be a victim. And it was well past the point of doing anything about her sister and Carlos. They'd been married eighteen months. She didn't know if her sister was any happier. She didn't know if Carlos was any happier. But she hated that he was on the property, even if not full-time. Even with her travels, she saw him too much when she was on the property.

She wished they would leave—move elsewhere. She would have cheerfully run this place herself. Her father had never intended for his daughters to run the sanctuary; he'd only intended for his son to operate it, and Keith was so enthused about taking over Dad's place.

Her father had intended for managers to take care of it while his son and daughters all went off and had lives. It was her father's pet project, something he had started late in life, after his wife, their mother, had gotten up and walked away from them. And she'd walked, like literally walked, away from twin daughters who were only eleven. He'd been devastated, but not as much as the girls had been. Keith had clung to their father, and they'd been inseparable until his death.

Her mother was around, back and forth every once in a while. She'd come to the wedding, had laughed at the circumstances surrounding a single male who had gone from sister to sister and told Lilianna it was her fault. How she should have never let him go if she really wanted him. That she had to learn to fight for what she wanted.

Harsh words, hurtful words and certainly not what Lilianna needed to hear back then. Her mother and her sister, so much alike, had bent heads together and twittered their way through the days of Mom's visit, once again making Lilianna feel lost and alone.

With her father's mental decline, she felt more alone than ever. It was hardly fair that the person she loved most in the world was suffering so much. He wasn't even that old, and she really wanted him to be alive and well for a long time.

But, after Keith's death, they'd all suffered. Her sister had been affected, but she had snapped out of it easily. Or maybe she hadn't. Maybe this frantic activity that she'd thrown herself into was a way to distract herself from missing her brother.

It had been a trying time for all of them. And things hadn't improved in the ensuing years. But all the issues now were like an underground rumor rising into a swell of public nastiness against the sanctuary. Her sister refused to believe any of it was even happening.

As far as Carlos was concerned, Lilianna was delicate and making a big deal out of nothing. Brianna had taken his side, loving that take on Lilianna's behavior. And Lilianna had found it beyond difficult to deal with either of them. She wanted Carlos to disappear and to take her sister with him.

But that was just small-minded thinking. It wasn't who she really was. Because, honestly, what she wanted was her father back home again. She just didn't know how to help him.

The men came downstairs as she drained the pasta. She glanced at them. "Run out of pins already?" she teased.

Liam flashed her a bright grin. Something was so authentic about that smile that it really hit home.

She shook her head at him. "You better turn the charm down. Women might get the wrong idea."

"Women *plural?*" he asked, looking around. "Don't tell me you have a triplet hidden away somewhere?"

She laughed. "I don't think I could handle that," she admitted. "Being a twin is tough enough."

"But being a twin is supposed to be special," Liam said. "And we work closely with one guy who's a twin."

She thought about the names Logan had spoken of and nodded. "Merk and Terkel, right?"

He nodded.

"Yes," North said.

"Both good men," Liam added. "Both very strong men and very close."

"*Really* close?" she said wistfully. "I always thought twins were supposed to be like that, but it was never my experience."

The men sat on the couch. The cabin had a small table that would seat four, but, until she was ready to put the food out, there was no point in sitting there.

"They seem like it. But then, what were they like growing up? Who knows?" Liam admitted. "Terkel is ... different."

"Logan told me. He has some kind of strong intuition, a seer kind of guy."

"Something like that." Liam nodded and smiled. "Some people would say he was psychic."

She stopped and stared at him, wondering if he was joking or if he really believed in it.

But he stared back at her with a bland, knowing look.

She shrugged. "The thing is, I can't say I disbelieve that stuff. Enough odd cases are out there that I shake my head and wonder just what we know and what we don't know in life."

Liam nodded approvingly.

"Terkel saved our ass many times," North admitted. "If he tells us to go home and to stay home, we do."

She stared at him, astonished. "He does that?"

"Mostly because his brother works with us, and he always has this insider line to Merk, being his twin. So, if he tells Merk to not take a flight or to not go somewhere or that a job is bad news or how something unusual is heading our way, we listen."

She sighed. "Wouldn't that be nice to know ahead of time?"

"Not necessarily," Liam said. "My grandmother had the sight. She would say some pretty unnerving things to us. Not necessarily things we wanted to know."

She served up the pasta and the sauce. "Do you have an example?"

He chuckled. "Well, she told me on prom night that I wouldn't get the girl. That was pretty depressing."

She stared at him for a long moment, and then her laughter pealed out across the small room. "Wow. No, I can't say that would appeal."

"She also told my father to stay home when he was heading into work one morning. Said it was too dangerous. He tried to tell her that he'd be fine, and she told him to get his ass back in that house and to stay there, or she'd have something to say to him. He groaned, turned to his wife and said, 'What do you want me to do?' She took the phone from my father's hand and asked Nana for an explanation. When my mother was done listening, she turned her head to my father and said, 'You're staying home.' We found out later the factory where he worked had a gas leak. Seven men died."

Lilianna shook her head. "Oh, my goodness, that's horrible." It was hard to believe what she had heard on a rational level, yet it obviously had happened in Liam's family. His nana had saved his father's life. She sighed and slowly carried the plates to the table, stunned at how close he'd come to losing his father. "I bet nobody ever disbelieved your grandmother again," she said.

"No, and there's been a couple times when I had major decisions in my life that I called her up and asked her for advice," he said quietly. "In my family you don't joke around with something like that."

She nodded, bringing over the Parmesan cheese, and sat at the table. She motioned at the plates and said, "Enjoy."

She sprinkled cheese over her pasta, her mind consumed with what it would be like to have a grandmother who could see such things. "I thought the prom thing was bad enough but to know she could see something like that?" She just shook her head.

"You get used to it, in a way," Liam said. "But you never, ever take it for granted."

"Does Terkel have that kind of ability?" Lilianna's gaze went from one man to the next.

They nodded.

"Wow." She picked up a forkful of pasta and tasted it. It wasn't bad. Maybe not her best but, given the circumstances, they were lucky to get a meal. She chuckled. "Like I said, I'm a plain cook. But I'm not a terrible one."

North's mouth was full. He looked at her with a sense of joy on his face. When he finally managed to empty his mouth, he said, "This is excellent. If you can cook like this, you've got no reason to feel bad."

From Liam came nothing but a murmur and a nod as he dug in.

And then she realized … "I should have thought about you missing lunch," she exclaimed. "Chocolate cake doesn't go far if you guys didn't get a full meal."

Liam held up a hand. "We were fine. Alfred fed us well this morning before we left and sent us with a full basket for the trip."

"That sounds wonderful," she said wistfully. "You're all one big happy family."

And seeing the odd look in their eyes, she dropped her gaze and focused on her meal. She wanted to be part of a big happy family. But somehow it didn't seem to work. "After dinner I'll visit my father," she announced. She hadn't seen him in a couple days anyway. It was hard to believe she was as homesick as she was, but she missed him in a big way.

"Good. May we come?" Liam asked.

She frowned, twirling her fork into the spaghetti noodles and shrugged. "I guess so."

"What's his condition like?"

"Lost in his own grief," she said shortly. "I'm not sure if there's a medical reason for it, but he's kind of in a stupor. He doesn't care about anything around him."

"Was there just the three of you kids?"

She nodded. "Yes, just the three of us. And he blames himself for Keith's death. I think the guilt and the grief collapsed this big man into this shell. He sits in a chair and doesn't care anymore. He's waiting for his life to end so he can join his son."

"What about his two daughters who need him?"

She gave him a half smile. "He would say that Brianna doesn't need anybody and that I'll do fine."

"But you're hurting too, aren't you?" Liam asked.

She refused to look at him. That question was a little too intuitively right on target.

She couldn't finish her dinner. Whether it was nerves or the shock of everything going on, she'd served herself too much food. She put down her fork and nudged her plate back a little. "I can't eat anymore," she said quietly.

"Stress will do that to you," North said. "Who draws a paycheck here?"

"It didn't used to be any of us," she said shortly. Then

she sighed and sagged. "The trouble is, I can't sustain myself without some income, and I spend all my time trying to raise money for the sanctuary. And my sister didn't use to take a paycheck, but, after she married Carlos, she started to."

"Well, somebody has to be paid to look after it," Liam said reasonably. "If you think about it, it'll be you, or it'll be somebody else coming in to manage it."

She nodded. "It's hard though when you realize you're having trouble getting money to look after the animals. If I could cut my salary any further I would. But I'm only taking $500 a month, and that's barely enough to cover my own personal needs."

"What does that mean?" North asked, leaning forward. "If you seriously get in trouble, what happens then?"

She stared at him and frowned. "I guess it means I have to sell some land. But I can't really do that without my father's permission."

"Do you have power of attorney?"

"I do for his medical care."

"Do you know for sure that Brianna hasn't tried to get a POA for the estate and sanctuary on her own?" North asked.

She stared at the men, both with questioning looks on their faces, and felt something rotten twist inside. "I hope not," she said quietly. "Because that would be the end of a very fragile trust between us."

LIAM WATCHED THE emotions crossing Lilianna's face. He wondered if she had any idea just how expressive her face was. She would never make a decent poker player. Right now she was completely sick over the thought of her sister pulling a fast one on her.

"We need to know a clear delegation as to who has access to the money, who has access to the website, who has access to the business documentation. Everything," North said.

Liam nodded. "And we need that fast." He watched her mouth work as if she wanted to say something.

Her shoulders sagged, and she nodded. "My understanding is my sister and I both have access to everything," she said quietly. "As does my father."

"Does that also mean Carlos does?" North said.

She shrugged. "There's no way to know what the hell Carlos knows."

"Is he honest? Is he somebody you trust with business?"

Her eyes were shadowed as she lifted them. "I was prepared to marry the man," she said quietly. "I thought for sure he was all of those things. But when you walk in to find your sister and your fiancé in bed together, you realize you really don't know either of them at all."

"Do you have any reason to believe he might be criminally connected? Maybe have an ulterior motive? Be after the property?"

Her eyes widened. "It never occurred to me before," she said. "He got what he wanted, which was my sister."

"Any idea why he wanted her over you?" Liam asked, his tone low. "I don't mean to make that sound terrible, but honestly, outside of love, do you think there's another reason?"

She shrugged. "I don't think so. As far as I know, he's wealthy and a good catch. I would have suspected it was more my sister after him because he was mine and because he had money."

Both men nodded as if they understood that. Liam certainly did. Women like that were all over the world. He was sorry for Lilianna's pain, but obviously she was better off without him.

"Anyone else have access to bank accounts, legal documents? Do you have a lawyer on staff?"

She shook her head. "Not on staff but we do have two professionals that we work with."

The men nodded, and North said, "We need those names too then."

She walked to her laptop and brought it to the kitchen table. "I've left a lot of the business stuff to my sister," she admitted. "I haven't really looked into it too deeply. I just wanted to avoid both of them."

"Who pays you?"

"The accountant. He deposits the money as per my instructions in my account."

"And what does your sister take from the business?"

She gave him a troubled look. "I'm not sure."

He leaned forward. "It's time to find out."

It was never an easy thing to look at those you worked with, particularly if they were family, to understand just what was going on. But mismanagement of funds was an all-too-common practice. Charities and animal sanctuaries were not exempt. And, if her sister was after the bottom line, maybe she felt the sanctuary owed her for looking after it. True enough, people did have to run it. The salary just needed to be a reasonable amount. She sent him a list of names and occupations in an email, then looked up and said, "Okay, that's done."

He nodded. "Let's go see your father."

She sighed. "I wish it *was* my father we'll see," she said cryptically.

"Is he that far gone?"

She raised both hands, palms up. "I have no idea. Seems to me the medication he is on is keeping him that way. But I can't get anybody to talk to me."

"Well, this time you won't be alone," Liam said in a curt tone. "Let's talk to your father and to his medical professionals. And let's see if anybody has changed his medication."

"Can they do that without informing me?" She glanced at him in surprise. "I'd imagine they could make minor changes without consulting me, but anything more wouldn't be allowed. Yet I have no idea. It would be horrific to think somebody was sabotaging not just the sanctuary but my father's health too."

"We have seen much worse," North said shortly. He collected their plates, filled the sink with hot soapy water and washed the dishes. "Go get whatever you need. We'll take our truck and visit your dad."

"Fine," she said, her tone also sharp.

Something else Liam could understand. He watched as she stalked off to her room. He cleared off the table and joined North to dry the dishes. Liam shook his head. Who wanted to take a look at everything going on in their lives in this kind of a way? He trusted what he could see and what he'd learned about Lilianna. But Brianna hadn't been welcoming, interested or compassionate about the animals.

And any asshole engaged to one sister who turned around and slept with the other wasn't somebody Liam would trust either. Liam knew, for a lot of men, sex was just that, sex. It didn't go with honor, love or commitment. That wasn't the world Liam lived in. As far as he was concerned, he was with one person until he was no longer with that person. But he never crossed the line between multiple partners.

Within ten minutes the kitchen was cleaned, and they were walking out to the truck. It was still light outside. Liam got into the driver's seat, and she hopped into the bed of the truck again.

He glanced over at North, but North just said, "She'll open the gate apparently."

Liam shook his head. "We could have done that."

"I think it's her way of distancing herself from all this."

Something else he could understand.

At the gate, she did indeed hop out, open the gate, let them out and closed it behind them. And then she sat in the back seat of the truck and gave directions to her father's assisted-care home.

A good twenty minutes later Liam pulled into the parking lot. He saw a lot of vehicles and a lot of people moving in and out.

"It's visiting hours," she said.

He nodded but didn't say a word. He studied the area, quickly typed the name of the place in a text to Levi. As far as Liam was concerned, something very wrong was going on. Anybody who saw the elephants probably thought they didn't need as much land as they had and didn't know about the expansion in the works. Or maybe knew about the intended expansion and was determined to thwart it. It wasn't fertile land, but land was land, and some of it held a great deal of value.

He glanced at her as they walked in. "I don't suppose your land has any oil or water or mineral rights or anything?"

She looked at him in surprise. "Well, we have a lake, a couple actually, from underwater springs. It's a beautiful spot."

"You'll have to show it to me," he said noncommittally, keeping his raging thoughts under control.

She nodded. "We can go out tomorrow if you want. It's pretty stunning back there."

"And when you say, *back there*, what does that mean?"

"It's at the far back corner of the property. We've had developers ask us about it, but my father was adamant about not selling. We need the water for the animals."

Liam glanced at North to see a look in his eyes and knew he was thinking too that *developers* included all kinds of people.

Inside the assisted-care home, Lilianna didn't sign-in or talk to the front desk; she just headed for her father's room.

"Is there no sign-in policy here? People just come and go at will?"

Surprised, she looked at him and nodded. "Of course. He's not a prisoner."

Liam wondered about that, but he kept quiet. Because, in reality, if the man had been drugged in any way, it probably *was* a prison for him.

She knocked on the door, opened it and stepped inside. Her father had a private room with a small couch, TV and a bed off to one side. As Liam looked at the man in front of him, he realized he wasn't all that old. In a low tone he asked, "How old is your father?"

"Fifty-nine," she said shortly. She stepped forward and, in a gentle voice, said, "Hi, Daddy. How are you?"

Hearing her voice, the man smiled gently. "Hello, Brianna. Back again so soon?"

She shook her head and sat down. "It's Lilianna, Dad. Not Brianna."

He patted her hand gently. "So you keep saying."

She glanced over at Liam and shrugged. "This is pretty common."

"Of course it is," he said. "You're identical twins."

Her father turned to look at him, but there was almost a vacant no-one's-home sign in the man's eyes. Liam stepped forward and held out his hand. "I'm Liam, a friend of your daughter's."

She nudged him when he didn't make a move. "Daddy, did you hear him?" She turned to Liam and smiled. "Liam, this is my father, Jim Howell. Daddy, this is Liam O'Brien."

Her father nodded and, at her urging, lifted a hand and shook Liam's. They repeated the process with North. But there was nothing cognizant going on in his gaze. Liam took a look around the room. No pill bottles sat on the bedside table where he could easily walk over and check them out. He really wanted to find out what kind of drugs this man was on. He glanced over at North, but he was already heading to the small bathroom. Liam could hear him checking out the insides of the cabinets and the drawers. When he returned, he stopped at the night table and did a quick glance through those drawers too. Lilianna watched what they were doing. She frowned, not quite understanding.

Just then a nurse walked in and stopped. "There you are," she said with a bright smile. "Haven't seen you in a couple of days."

Lilianna nodded. "How are you doing, Mary?"

"I'm doing fine, and so is your father, as you can see."

"What medication is he on?" Liam asked.

Mary's smile dimmed. She turned to study Liam and obviously didn't like either the tone or the look of him because her back stiffened. "If you have any questions about his medications, then you need to talk to his doctor."

"I'd love to," he said smoothly. "Who is his doctor, and how do I contact him?"

She hesitated and glanced at Lilianna. "Lilianna?"

Lilianna studied Mary's face. "I have no problem with Liam understanding my father's care. Do you?"

The woman blushed slightly and shook her head. "Of course not. I'll get you the information." And then she disappeared.

North stepped out of the room following the nurse. Lilianna turned toward Liam and, in a harsh whisper, asked, "Do you really think something is wrong here?"

"Your father needs a second medical opinion," Liam said softly, staring at Jim who sat gazing almost blandly at the TV. "I want a reasonable explanation for what happened to him and why he's like this."

She studied her father, gripped his fingers and said, "Daddy, how has your day been?"

He shifted his gaze toward her and then back at the TV again. To Liam nothing was normal about this. But unless the man had an aneurism or a stroke or was dealing with early-onset Alzheimer's, Liam didn't understand what was going on. Yet it was all too possible this was who this man was now. In which case, Liam could easily see somebody trying to get a power of attorney over his estate. That's where the money was. It was smart for Lilianna to have POA over her father's medical needs, but Liam was worried that she should have POA over the rest as well.

The nurse came back with a name and an email address on a piece of paper that she handed to Liam. "If you have any other questions, please direct them to the home care director."

Liam brought out a pen. "Absolutely. Who do I contact?"

She gave him the information and turned to Lilianna. "You want some tea?"

Lilianna nodded. "Is Dad drinking any still?"

She shrugged. "Last time I brought some, it was left untouched."

"We'd like to have a cup of tea now then, please."

The nurse turned and left.

Liam pulled out his phone, walked to the window and called Levi. As soon as he answered, Liam said, "You need to check into the medical records of Jim Howell, Lilianna's father. I'm at the assisted-care home where he's staying. He's not talking, walking or acting normally, as if he's drugged or has early-onset dementia or Alzheimer's. He's sitting in the chair doing nothing. The man's only fifty-nine. I highly suspect we'll find somebody is trying for power of attorney over the estate behind Lilianna's back." He caught Levi's indrawn breath and a light swearing.

"I'm on it. I'm also calling Gunner. He might have more info."

"It's the medical that worries me right now. It's a little too easy to keep him in this state to prove he's not capable of handling his business affairs. No judge would argue a POA application for the estate given the condition I'm seeing Jim in now. He's not capable of handling his business affairs."

"We're on it."

Liam put his phone away and returned to where Lilianna sat beside her father. Tears were in her eyes.

Just then the door opened as the nurse came back in with a tray.

Liam said to Lilianna, "Levi is checking into the POA

issue."

The nurse hurriedly put down the tray. "It has nothing to do with us," she cried. "You have to talk to the director." And she dashed out.

"Time to call that lawyer," Liam said pointedly to Lilianna.

She stared at him in shock.

Chapter 4

H ER FINGERS SHAKING, Lilianna pulled out her phone and ran through her contacts, looking for the lawyer's information. As soon as she found it, she hit Dial. When Eric answered, she said, "Did you draw up a power of attorney for my father's estate?"

There was silence on the other end.

"You did, didn't you?" she cried out.

"Your sister asked me to. But we haven't signed anything yet," Eric protested. "You were looking after your father's medical condition. She wanted to handle the business side. Said it was only right as she's been handling that side since your father's collapse anyway."

"Well, let me tell you, if you go forward with that, without out involving me in this discussion, there will be a lawsuit against you," she snapped, her anger thick.

"Now I just said we haven't gotten that far," he protested.

"But you've started the process, and that means you've done it without my knowledge," she said, fear working through her. "As of this moment, you are no longer a lawyer for us, the family or the sanctuary. Do you understand me?"

"Now hold on a minute …"

"No, you'll be hearing from my new attorneys tomorrow morning," she snapped and hung up. She dropped the phone in her lap and brushed the hair off her face, but her hands trembled so badly that she dropped them into her lap and just left them there. "I've been a fool, haven't I?"

"I think what we're seeing here is a power play," North said quietly. "I suspect your sister and her husband are making a move to take control, and you will end up as an employee at a measly $500 a month doing all the work so they can do whatever it is they've got going on."

She shook her head. "Are you seriously thinking something has happened with my father here?"

"I'm seriously thinking you should have gotten a second opinion a long time ago," Liam said bluntly.

The color washed out of her face. As she stared at him, guilt ripped through her. "The doctors all told me nothing could be done, that this was just who he was, and he'd either pull out of it, or he wouldn't."

"And what do you think about that now?"

She shook her head. "It's one thing to think my sister is making a play for the property behind my back," she said, speaking slowly, carefully. "It's another thing entirely to think somebody is either not giving my father full professional medical care or deliberately keeping him in this state."

"We also want to see the report on your brother's death."

She gasped and fell back on the couch beside her father, staring at the two men. She shook her head. "No, no. Don't go there."

"We have to," Liam said gently. He sat beside her and picked up her icy-cold fingers. "Your brother didn't deserve to die. Your father does not deserve this." He motioned to the man sitting vacantly beside them. "All sorts of drugs can bring on this kind of stupor. It's hardly fair to the vibrant man he used to be."

Just then Liam's phone rang. He pulled it out. "I have to take this call," he said quietly. "Levi? What's up?" She stared at him, haunted as he moved a foot away to talk. First thing he did was to tell Levi about the lawyer.

She stared as bits and pieces of the conversation floated around her.

"Okay. I'll tell you this. You'll have to contact the facility tomorrow morning and make sure no roadblocks pop up."

Then Liam stopped and turned to look in her direction. He spoke again. "Right. Okay, good. If Gunner gets on this, maybe we can get some action too."

It was just too much to grasp. The last thing she wanted was to hear there had been foul play in her brother's death. As she stared at her father, she realized the decline had been so slow that she hadn't seen it. Not until someone new came on site to see him. She'd been so caught up in her own sadness and worry that she hadn't seen how quickly her father was declining. She grabbed his hand gently and said, "We'll do everything we can."

"And that'll start tomorrow morning," Liam said in a hard voice. "We have a specialist involved now. He'll take a look at your father's condition and medications."

"He is coming here?"

Liam shook his head. "Not if we don't need him to. We'll send your father's medical records to him to examine. But if there are any legal or corporate complications, he will come here. Gunner has also been informed, and he's pretty pissed off. As of this moment, Gunner's lawyer is representing the sanctuary and you."

She sagged in place. "You know my sister will have a shit fit when she finds out."

He nodded. "It'll be a legal fight, depending on how far along they are in the process. Whose name is on the land?"

She stared at him. "My father's and my brother's. But, with my brother's death, that left my father as sole owner."

"Why your brother?"

"He was supposed to take over running the sanctuary. This was his life."

"And now we're back to wanting the report on your brother's death."

"There was an investigation," she said quietly. "It was an accident, but there had to be an official investigation regardless." She thought about it for a long moment. "Detective Olson. He's the man I spoke to. He should be able to help you." She watched as Liam typed a text, sending it off as she heard a tone. "Are you guys always this fast?"

Liam shot her a hard look. "Absolutely. And now we are running out of time. If people are getting paperwork signed and sealed behind your back, we have to put legal stops in place."

"How fast can that happen?"

He gave her a glance. "You can bet there will be shit happening before tomorrow morning."

She shuddered. "Will they need my signature on anything?"

He nodded. "Do you have a scanner at home? Do you know a notary?"

"Everyone is closed by now," she cried out. "My printer is a scanner though."

"Do you have any protection for your cabin?"

She stared at him. "What are you talking about?"

"What if somebody stole your computer equipment and destroyed it so, when you got home, you couldn't access your data much less print or scan anything?"

"That's a scary thought." She paled.

He nodded and glanced over at North. "We should get our laptops."

North nodded. "They are in the truck."

"Good. Sounds like we need them."

Just when she thought things could not get any crazier, a knock came on her father's door. A stranger walked in with a serious look on his face. "I'm looking for Liam O'Brien."

Liam stepped forward. "That's me."

The man shook his hand. "I'm the director of this facility. I've just been contacted at home and had to come back into work."

Liam nodded, but his face gave nothing away.

She watched from one man to the other, then asked, "Who called you in?"

The director gave her a shuttered look. "Lawyers."

"Good," she said. "Because it sounds like shit is happening behind my back with my father, and that is not cool."

He stared at her for a long moment. "And you are?"

Her eyebrows shot up. "I'm Lilianna Howell."

He nodded. "Do you have ID?"

She stood slowly. "Why?"

"Because we can't prove you are who you are when you have an identical twin sister."

"Are you saying my sister might have tried to impersonate me?"

He just stared at her and said, "ID please."

She opened her purse, pulled out her wallet and brought out her driver's license.

He glanced at it and nodded. "Having twin sisters and their father in the hospital with a large estate and control over a big elephant sanctuary can create all kinds of difficulties."

"But this isn't about the property," she said gently. "This is about my father's medical care."

"We certainly haven't done anything except give him the best care possible," he said in an equally deceptively mild tone. "And any accusations to the contrary won't be tolerated."

Liam stepped between the two of them. "It depends if we find that anything untoward has occurred. But that's part of our investigation," he said calmly. "I'd like your ID now too please."

Without a word the director pulled out his wallet and handed over his driver's license. Liam took a photo of it and then typed on his phone for a few minutes.

"What are you doing?" the director asked.

"Sending it for verification and a criminal background check," Liam said calmly.

The director stiffened. "I don't understand what brought this on," he said, his voice easing into something less aggressive.

"Her father's condition for one," Liam said curtly.

The director glanced at her father who sat there staring at the TV. The director frowned and crouched in front of her father. "Jim, how are you today?"

Her father didn't respond. The director turned toward her. "What was he like the last time you saw him?"

"The same."

The director shrugged and stood. "So why are you expecting him to be any different today?"

"Because he wasn't like this a few months ago," she snapped. "And I'm not sure that anything has been done to help him, outside of keeping him drugged to make it easier on you people."

"You know your father had an incident not all that long ago where he was aggressive and difficult. He assaulted a nurse if you recall."

She frowned at him. "I was never told about that," she said. "When was this?"

"Of course you were told," he said. "This is the problem we have with family. They remember what they want to remember, and they forget the rest."

"Or, in this case, potentially the wrong sister was told," North said, stepping forward. "As you can't tell one sister from the other, that's quite a possibility."

"That doesn't make it our fault," the director said, his voice stiff again. "If we told you in good faith, then our responsibility has been taken care of."

"And what happened to him after that incident?" Liam asked, once again stepping in.

Good thing because she was thrown for a loop and didn't know how to proceed. She sat beside her father, picked up his hand and gently stroked it. "The only reason he would have fought a nurse was if he thought he was in danger."

"I don't see how that could be unless he was hallucinating. He's very safe here. We've given him the best of care," the director said. "I understand it's painful to see a loved one like this. But that doesn't make it our fault."

"Then you won't have a problem handing over his medical records to a specialist who will take a look and determine a future treatment plan."

The director frowned. "It would have to go through formal channels."

Lilianna snorted. "I'm family. I am entitled to see what he's been given, what he's currently being given and who placed those orders."

The director stared at her for a moment. "Let me see what I have." He pivoted and walked out.

She turned to Liam. "Is this for real? And what does this have to do with the charity money drying up?"

"I'd say there's sabotage. And you need to prepare yourself. Your sister could be behind it."

She shook her head. "My sister is selfish and very focused on what she wants, but I would never have said she was involved in something as criminal as this."

"What about her husband?" North said. "Would she do what he asked her to do?"

Lilianna stared at the two men, wanting to shut down her mind and to walk away from this whole mess, but she couldn't do that. Not when her father's life was at stake. "I don't think she would do it just because he asked." She tried to think her way through understanding her sister's mentality. "She might do it if she believed in it. If he could turn her to his way of thinking, then that's possible."

"So then you have to ask yourself, is this really what's right for your father? And, if you had any doubts, why did you not get another opinion?"

"Because we didn't think there was any need," she said painfully. "I trusted the doctors here."

"And it's possible they haven't done anything wrong," Liam said. "It's also possible they haven't done the best by him either."

Just then the director returned. He had a tablet in his hand, flicking through it. He said, "This is your father's medical records. He's been here for two years and has had a steady decline in his condition."

"Why is that?" Liam said.

"Who's to say? Anyway, it's psychological. The loss of his son affected him greatly. He stepped out of life and has no wish to return."

"Are you giving him any drugs to keep him calm and less aggravated?"

The doctor flicked through several pages and then nodded. "Yes. After the attack on the nurse, he was given drugs to keep him calmer. We can't have any of the staff here being injured as they look after him."

"Send me a copy of that file please," Liam said. "I want it emailed, and I'm sending it on to a specialist."

"If you're saying our care has been any less than exemplary ..." the director said.

"I'm saying that," Lilianna snapped. "I'm quite pissed. I have POA over his medical care, and I wasn't informed." She still couldn't get her head wrapped around the idea that her sister might have impersonated her, but it didn't let the director off the hook if he informed the wrong person. She jumped to her feet and paced, her anger and fear driving her forward.

The director looked at her. "My understanding was you agreed to his medical plan."

Lilianna spun to stare at him. "No. Apparently my sister did."

Liam held her by the shoulders. "Calm down. We'll get to the bottom of this. We have lawyers already on it. Remember that."

The director stared at the two of them. "We don't want to get between family disputes. Our job here is to give our patients the best care we can."

"Which you failed miserably at," North said. "Have you tried any other treatments, brought in any other specialists, to see about his condition?

"Our staff members are specialists in their fields," the director said, his nose in the air. "I don't know why, all of a sudden, you've decided we're some sort of criminal unit here. We do care about our patients."

"Yes, but I guess the question really is," Lilianna said, "do you care more about some than others? And do you take payouts to turn your eye? A great deal of money is to be made off my family's property if somebody gets power of attorney over my father's estate because of his condition. A condition that appears to have degenerated until you've completely zombied him."

The director gave her a hard look and nodded to the men. "Our lawyers are always available to speak with you." And he turned and walked out.

Liam looked at her and chuckled. "*Zombied?*"

HE LOVED TO see the fire inside her. Too often people became almost apathetic in a situation they didn't know how to get out of. But now that she realized something was going on, she'd found her fighting spirit.

North's phone went off. He walked to the corner of the room.

Liam sat on the couch beside Lilianna. "You aren't obligated to keep him here if you want to move him."

"And where do I move him?" she asked wearily. "I need a specialist to go over his medical records and to determine if he's been given the best care possible. At least he's here, close, and I can come and visit him often."

"How often does your sister come?"

"I don't know," she said. "I've never seen her here. I assumed she wasn't coming at all."

"I wonder if I can find that out," he said. "Stay here with North. I'll be back in a few minutes." He walked down the hall to the reception area. "Do you have a sign-in book for guests?"

The nurse looked up at him. "No, we don't."

He nodded. "So do you have any idea how often Brianna comes in to see her father?"

"The two women look so much alike, I have no idea. For all I know it's always one or the other. There's no way to tell."

He nodded. "That's what I thought."

She glanced at him and frowned. "Why?"

He gave her a ghost of a smile. "Because it appears one sister's trying to pull something over on the other."

The nurse frowned. Then she leaned forward. "I shouldn't be saying this, but I'm pretty sure it's always Lilianna who's here. Brianna wouldn't give us the time of day unless to give us shit if something was not the way she liked it. If she was here more often, I'm sure she'd be complaining. Lilianna is easy to get along with."

Liam nodded, leaned forward, slightly conspiratorially, and said, "That's what I kind of figured. Can't say Brianna struck me as being a very easygoing woman."

"I went to school with both of them," she said. "I was a couple years ahead, but Brianna was already making a name for herself. She was pretty difficult if she didn't get what she wanted."

"I'm sure you heard about the marriage issue," he said.

She rolled her eyes. "Yeah, we all felt sorry for Lilianna.

That's got to be a hard one. But then, if you ask me, she's better off without him."

"I haven't met him," Liam said, causing her smile to brighten and widen. "What's he like?"

"Slimy," she said. Then she flushed and glanced around the empty reception area. "But, if I get caught saying anything, I'm in trouble."

He nodded. "I hear ya. I might be getting some documents in to sign tonight. Do you have a fax here?"

She nodded. "I do." She wrote down the number. "If you need stuff faxed in, you can send it here and then sign it if you need to."

"Thanks, I'll see if they can do that right now." He walked back into the room to see North and Lilianna standing close, talking. As much as he really liked North, he didn't want to see him quite so near to the most interesting woman Liam had met in a long time.

"Any news?" he asked North.

"Documents are being drawn up right now. We need to get signatures though."

"The nurse at reception said we could fax to their machine. We can do the signatures there and send them back."

North pulled out his phone. "Then let's go to the reception area and do that." He held out his hand for the number, turned away to make a call.

Liam studied Lilianna. "You holding up okay?"

She looked tired and frustrated. "Presumably this has to go through a judge?"

He nodded. "I believe that's the way it has to go. But it could be just signatures and lawyers."

"Okay," she said. "Then I need to sign as fast as possible, especially if this is the only way to stop my sister from gaining that type of control over him."

Chapter 5

LILIANNA LOOKED AT the nurse at reception and said, "Katie, how are you doing tonight?"

Katie laughed. "I'm doing fine. I understand you might be in a spot of trouble though."

Lilianna grinned. "When am I not?"

Katie laughed. "How are the elephants?"

"They're about the only sane thing in my world right now," Lilianna said with a big grin. "They're happy. They're free. They've got space, food and water, and they're not chained up and living in cramped quarters."

"I really appreciate what you are doing for them," Katie said. 'I'd love to see you get more animals out there."

"It's under discussion," Lilianna said. "I just wish to God I could get my father back on his feet."

Katie nodded. Just then the fax machine behind her beeped. She got up as paper rolled through it. She read the cover sheet and turned to Lilianna. "This is page one of three for Lilianna and Liam." She turned and looked at Liam.

He nodded. "That's me."

Without looking at the documents, she pulled the rest of them off the machine and handed them over. Lilianna watched as Liam read through them. He leaned over, grabbed the pen off the reception desk and told Lilianna, "Sign here."

She gave the documents a quick glance and then signed. After she signed, he asked Katie to witness the signature. And then he said, "Can we send these back, please?"

Just as she dialed the number, the director came to the desk. "What's going on here?"

Liam turned to look at him. "We're sending out a fax."

He frowned, but the paper was already rolling through the machine. "I hope it has nothing to do with our earlier discussion."

"We deliberately kept you out of it because you didn't want to be involved in a family dispute, remember?" Liam said with a raised eyebrow.

The director gave a curt nod and left.

When the fax was sent and confirmed, Katie clipped together the cover sheet, the documents, and the confirmation of the fax having been sent and handed it over to Liam. "I hope that does what you need it to do," she said. "I hate to see families torn apart."

Lilianna grabbed Katie's fingers and gave them a squeeze. "You always were a sweetheart."

Katie shook her head. "So not true. If that was the case, I'd be married with three kids by now."

Lilianna stopped and looked at her. "I remember you were in a pretty hot and heavy relationship with Larry. What happened to that?"

Katie frowned. "He left me at the altar," she said. "Took off with my bridesmaid."

Lilianna gasped.

Katie raised her gaze. "And I know that you know how that feels."

The two women stared at each other in mutual commiseration.

Liam wrapped an arm around Lilianna's shoulders and nudged her toward her father's room. He glanced over at Katie and whispered, "Thanks."

She gave him a big smile.

As they walked down the hall, Lilianna said, "That's so not fair. Katie is such a sweetie."

"Do you trust her?"

Lilianna nodded. "Absolutely. As much as I do anyone."

Liam had to think about that because she seemed to be way too trusting, very innocent in so many ways. "Do you think she would have taken money to hide or falsify records or done anything to keep your father in that condition?"

"I would hope not," Lilianna admitted. "She never did like my sister."

"Sounds like not too many people did."

"No," Lilianna said. "I always felt like I had to be overly nice to make up for my sister's bitchiness."

"Not your job," Liam said.

"It doesn't matter though, does it?" Lilianna said. "Our roles were set a long time ago."

He shook his head. "Doesn't have to be that way now. You get to change that status quo at any time."

He opened the door to her father's room and stepped inside; she walked in and sat down beside her father. "I really don't want to leave you tonight, Dad."

But he stared at her without any sign of recognition.

She glanced at North and said, "What do I do now?"

Just then the nurse came in. "Visiting hours are almost over." The new nurse bustled in with a cheerful smile. "It's time for his medication."

"His medication has been discontinued," Liam said. "We're letting him sleep off the dosage tonight."

The nurse looked at him in surprise. "Really?" She shrugged. "I'll ensure that's documented. I have to follow orders."

"Check with the director," Liam said. He glanced at Lilianna. "Do you want to stay here with him tonight?"

She was torn. "They've always taken good care of him. I can't see that they're actively trying to hurt him. But I really don't know anything about this new doctor."

"New doctor?"

She nodded. "I think it was about four months ago that he was assigned a new doctor."

"Any particular reason why?"

"Staff changes? Patient changes?" She shook her head. "Does anybody ever really know in a place like this?"

"Give us the name of the new one and the old one."

"But it's on the medical records. Why don't you ask Katie for more insider information," she said.

North said, "My turn. I'll ask her."

"Remember, her name is Katie," Liam said with a grin.

North's face broke into a charming smile. "Let me go make Katie's acquaintance."

Lilianna watched him go. "I almost feel sorry for her. You guys have lethal smiles. There should be a law against so much sex appeal in small spaces."

Liam stared at her as if she'd gone off her rocker.

She waved at him. "Don't even try to give me that look."

"What look?"

"The one that says you don't know what I'm talking about," she said with a laugh. "You use compliments and charm to get what you want."

"We all do, depending on the circumstances," he said. "And, in the current situation, we'll do whatever we need to do to look after your father and you and the property."

She stared at him, her heart sinking. "It's a little hard for me to consider that my sister is doing something so destructive."

"It's hard to say she is. I mean, if she saw your father attacking somebody, or heard about it from somebody who exaggerated it, it makes full sense she would want him sedated so nobody got hurt. Maybe she felt she had to do it with subterfuge as you'd never believe her or agree."

At that Lilianna turned to look at her father. "This isn't even a life."

"But there's certainly life left in him."

"How long before your specialist gets a chance to go through the medical records?"

"He's already got them," Liam said quietly. "As for how long to hear back, I don't know."

"Who is this man you sent them to?"

He glanced at her with a big grin. "Ice's father. The records went to him, and then he contacted a specialist."

She frowned. "An awful lot of people are getting involved." Her voice was hesitant. "I certainly don't have money for all that too."

"Of course not. A place like this can't be cheap."

She shook her head. "It's not. That's where my personal money has gone."

"So the sanctuary isn't paying for this?"

She shook her head. "Oh, goodness no. That wouldn't be fair. Father does have medical insurance, and that's covering eighty percent of it, but we're covering the other twenty."

He looked at her, his lips quirking. "Who's *we*?"

She sighed, her shoulders sagging. "Make that me."

"Well, it's not coming from the $500 you're getting from the charity," he said quietly. "So where else is it coming from?"

She frowned. "My brother's life insurance."

He stared at her in horror. "We're back to your brother and his accident again."

She nodded. "He left me a $75,000 life insurance policy. He left my sister a $50,000 one."

"Why the difference?"

"That's what Brianna has always asked me. But honestly the answer is simple. He didn't get along with her. She wasn't the nicest person in the family, and he knew it. He also knew I had spent a lot of my time letting her get away with shit and getting more out of basically everyone, but it was a surprise that he had life insurance at all."

"Does your father have a policy?"

She nodded. "He's got a $100,000 policy."

"Where is that?"

She looked at him in surprise. "Among the paperwork regarding his other legal assets, I presume. I never thought to ask."

"So there's a $100,000 life insurance policy that'll pay out upon Jim's death, plus the sanctuary property and whatever other assets your father might have, for whoever gets a general power of attorney?"

"But that general power of attorney doesn't mean you get to just grab whatever you want," she said. "My father needs care, and he's young. The sanctuary needs assistance too. I give it all the time I can for marketing and all the free labor I can for working onsite. Any general POA is to do what needs to be done."

Liam nodded. "Upon Jim's death, that sum won't last

more than a few years."

She frowned. "I'm not talking about that. That's many years down the line. I'm talking about what's needed now. What's available now to care for Dad. My thinking was we were clear for ten years between my brother's $75,000 life insurance and Dad's pension and his medical insurance"

"And why are you giving all your brother's inheritance toward Jim's medical care?"

She shrugged irritably. But she stayed silent.

"Because you felt guilty, right?"

She glared at him. "Well, it wasn't a very nice thing to realize your brother left one sister more than the other."

"It's your brother's life insurance. He can do whatever the hell he wants," Liam said forcibly.

"Fine, okay. So it's guilt. But I still can't keep my father like this forever."

Liam nodded. "Did the health insurance say anything about a time frame?"

She shook her head. "No, he always had very good health insurance. He was an engineer for a big telecommunications company. He had a very good pension with that. It was being paid directly into the sanctuary account. He wanted to make sure the elephants were fine no matter what. His health insurance was for the rest of his life."

"Good thing," Liam said. "Because this could end up being a long-term thing."

"You're kidding me, right? It *is* a long-term thing."

Just then Liam's phone rang. He looked at the Caller ID and walked to the other side of the room to talk. "Levi, what's up?"

And that's all she could hear. Lilianna sat here, thinking about how off her world was. She didn't have anything against her sister, but Brianna wasn't anybody who necessarily cared beyond what she could see in front of her.

Brianna had been looking after the place since her brother's death. But, if Lilianna thought about all the things they had discussed that needed to be done that weren't getting done, she wondered just how much effort her sister had put into it. If any. And that was fairly disruptive too.

North walked in. He sat beside her. "Now I have the two doctors' names," he said cheerfully.

She looked at him suspiciously. "You were nice to Katie, right?"

He gave her a bland look. "Of course I was. She looks like a sweetheart."

There was enough truth in his voice that she relaxed. "She is, but, as I found out, nice girls don't always end up getting what they want or deserve."

"What do you want?"

She stared at him in surprise. "I want my father back on his feet—the same strong, healthy, robust man he was before my brother's death. I want the sanctuary to stay safe so those elephants have everything they need for the rest of their natural lives."

"That's great and all, but that has nothing to do with what you need for *you*."

"I really don't think about me. I'm all about everybody else."

He nodded. "I get that. But that's not always enough. You have needs too."

"Funny. After Carlos switched to my sister, I can't say I felt like I had very many needs. I went pretty numb for a while. With my brother, my father, and then my fiancé ..." She shook her head. "At the time I didn't think I'd trust another man again."

"But obviously you trusted Gunner," he said.

She nodded. "Gunner has always been good to me. He trusted my father, and my father trusted him. So, when trouble was brewing, I didn't know who else to go to."

She glanced at Liam in the corner of the room, still on the phone, and back to North. "You do realize none of this has to do with the website, the bad-mouthing, the ugly news reports, the loss of donations?"

"That's not true," North said. "We'll probably find it's a big smear campaign. At least it would appear so at one level. Yet it's almost always about power, money or sex behind it all."

"It seems so sad to think that everything in life boils down to those few elements."

"What would you like to see life boil down to?" North asked.

She stared at him for a long moment, then smiled. "How about love? Honesty? Truth? Honor?" She kept tossing them out, and he kept nodding. "Is it really so hard to have that?" she asked.

"No, not at all," he said. "And sometimes I think that we're a minority because both Liam and I think the same way you do. But a lot of the world doesn't."

"My brother was like me," she said softly. "He was gentle. The elephants were his life. My father was very much like that. My mother not so much."

"How often do you see your mother?"

She shook her head. "Not often. At my sister's wedding, then about five months ago."

"Sounds like that was enough."

She gave him a lopsided grin. "My mother told me how

it was my fault I lost my fiancé. If I had been better in bed, he wouldn't have had to go to my sister. And that my sister was obviously a way better woman than I was."

He stared at her.

Her lips twisted. "Right? So do I need that again?" She shook her head. "No, I don't."

"What does your mother do?"

"Marries well," she said, and then a laugh burst free. "I didn't mean to say that."

"Well, you did," North said. "And it's an interesting statement. Do you want to elaborate?"

She shrugged. "What I mean is, she marries well, gets wealth from her marriages and moves up."

"How many times has she been married?"

"Three times. My father was the first."

"Is she's still married?"

"No. She's currently looking for number four."

"Divorces?"

"With my father, yes. Husband number two, no. He died in a car accident. Husband number three"—she frowned—"I don't remember. I think she caught him in an affair, and they divorced, but I'm not sure. It's unclear. I think she got a huge payout because he was this big business name, and she got hush money to not make a scene."

"That would make sense," he said. "She's looking for number four, now that she's done with the last two."

"Oh, she's done well out of all three," she said. "My father had lots of money. She made sure she got a decent portion of it."

"And of course she's not pitching in for his health care now, right?" His tone said he knew what the answer was.

"Does any ex ever help the person they supposedly loved

at one time?"

"I've seen it happen," North said. "But not very often."

Just then Liam joined them and said, "Ice has been talking to her father. He's brought in a neurosurgeon and their psychiatrist. They've all had an online conference discussing treatment for your father." He sat down hard beside them. "How do you feel about handing him over to Ice's father for a few weeks to see if they can do something with him?"

"Did they say what's brought this on?"

"They said it does happen sometimes. People get so caught up in grief that they shrink inside, but, until the drugs are out of his system, we won't know what his true mental state is like."

She said, "Will I get him there, or will that be a legal fight?"

"Nothing in the medical records says you can't pull him out," Liam said. "But, if you're interested, you would have to go to California. That's where Ice's father is."

"He can't travel that distance," Lilianna said softly. "Is there anybody here who can treat him?"

"That was the next option," Liam said. "They are looking for another colleague who might take it on. They'll get back to us by morning."

She sighed. "But we can still stop his medication now, right?"

"Absolutely. All three doctors agreed on that. They said it could take forty-eight hours for the drugs to completely withdraw from his system, but there'd be an improvement within eight hours. And, if you're at all concerned that he might turn aggressive, then it's suggested we stay here."

"All of us?" she asked, astonished.

"No," Liam said. He looked over at North. "Levi and

Gunner want to make sure one of us goes back to the cabin."

"Why?" she demanded. She hopped to her feet, pacing. "This is bizarre, all of it."

"True enough, but you left your laptop and paperwork there. We've got gear there. We just want to make sure everything is safe."

North shrugged. "I can run back up, strip out the cabin if you want? You stay here with Lilianna. Let's get Jim into bed, considering the lateness of the hour. Make sure he's not given any more medications, and you two can stand watch over him. I'll be back early in the morning to see what the plan is, how Jim is then."

"Stay and sleep at the cabin," Liam said. "We can call you in the morning if and when we find out anything, or you can call us."

Lilianna looked at her watch. "It's almost ten o'clock. What if they try to kick us out?"

"Not likely. Ice's father just contacted the director. It's been agreed we should stay here with him."

"And if something happens, and he reacts in an odd way?"

"There will be night staff and doctors on call," Liam said. "What we want to make sure is that whatever is keeping him in this stupor drains from his system so we have a chance to evaluate what his condition really is."

"Are we suggesting somebody might come in during the night and drug him with more or try to wait for us to leave?"

"The thing is, we don't know," Liam said. "We don't know anything. Yet."

North hopped to his feet. "It's already ten past ten." He turned to look at Lilianna. "Is there anything else I should collect for you? Do you have documentation, a purse, money, weapons?"

It took her a long moment to really understand what he was asking. "Yes," she said, suddenly very weary. "There's a handgun under my pillow. There is money underneath the bottom mattress. I have electronics. And documentation, like my passport, bank account information are in my file drawer."

He nodded. "I'll make sure it's safe." He glanced at Liam. "Watch your back."

She watched the two men exchange glances as she tried to figure out what the hell was going on.

Then Liam said, "You watch yours."

And North walked out.

She looked at Liam for a long moment. "Surely no one would attack us here? This is like a hospital, with three shifts of nurses and doctors. Witnesses all around. Plus we are healthy, can defend ourselves."

He shot her a hard look. "What we don't know is why this is happening. We'll plan on a peaceful night with both of us getting rest, but we'll also ensure nobody comes in to keep your father sedated. What I'd like to know and I couldn't find in the medical files, and nobody else could either, is what brought on his sudden aggressiveness."

"Oh, I never thought of that," she said in confusion. "Surely something was written in the records?"

"There is a note that he turned aggressive, but it doesn't say why." He flicked through his phone. "It also says you were here earlier that night, but after you left was when he got angry."

She shook her head, bewildered. "I don't remember anything about that."

"If it happened *after* you left, you wouldn't, would you?"

he asked reasonably.

A nurse knocked and came in. "Your father needs to go to bed now, Lilianna."

Lilianna smiled and nodded. "He's already in his pajamas. Does he get dressed in the daytime at all?"

The nurse shrugged. "I don't know. I deal with him at night on my shifts."

The nurse helped her father to his feet, took him to the bathroom. They could hear her voice as she murmured, telling him to brush his teeth. From what Lilianna could see, her father followed instructions perfectly.

Liam stood at the bathroom door. She wondered what he was doing, but he held a finger to his lips. His head tilted into the bathroom. Finally the nurse brought her father back out, his teeth brushed, his face washed, and she helped him in bed and pulled the covers over his shoulders.

The nurse glanced at the night table, then back at them. "I understand he isn't supposed to get his medication tonight, correct?"

Liam nodded. "That's correct."

She stared down nervously. "I don't know what his withdrawal symptoms will be like."

"If there's any problem we'll call you," Lilianna said. She sat beside her father on the chair next to his bed and gently stroked his hand. He lay in a prone position, his eyes already closed. "How does he eat these days?" She noted the skin sagging on his cheeks.

"He's not eating very much, but it's enough," the nurse said with a smile. "I was really hoping he'd pull out of this."

"Me too," Lilianna said. "It's so hard to see him like this."

"I know." The nurse patted Lilianna's shoulder. "If you

need me, let me know and I'll come."

Lilianna smiled. "Thanks."

The nurse went out and closed the door with a harsh *click*.

Lilianna glanced at Liam. "Now it's just us."

He nodded. "Will you lie down on the couch and sleep?"

She shook her head. "At least not now," she said honestly. "My mind is too wired."

"Right. Hopefully, as we get answers, you can relax."

Her phone buzzed. She pulled it out and sighed. "It's Brianna. What does she want?" She swiped her phone screen to unlock it and brought up her sister's text. "She's asking where I am."

"Tell her that you're out with me," he said.

"Why?" she asked, looking up at him.

"Because, if she thinks you're not home, she might break in."

"But won't she see North's truck?"

Liam checked his watch. "North should be pulling up in another five minutes or so. Can she see the lights of the truck as he drives in?"

"I guess if she was to walk up the rise. But part of the reason why the houses are where they are is for privacy."

He said, "I'll call North. I'll have him kill the lights and get the stuff out that's needed. I'll have him hide the truck behind the cabin."

"Are you serious?"

He nodded. "Don't answer her for a moment." He placed the call. North's voice filled his car.

She could just about hear him.

"North, where are you?"

"Just about at the turnoff."

"Kill the lights," Liam said urgently. "Brianna just texted Lilianna, asking where she is."

"DONE," NORTH SAID calmly. "Am I to expect a visitor, do you think?"

"I suspect so," Liam said. "Even more important is that you get whatever paperwork is there out beforehand."

"I'm driving slowly up and around the back now. I don't see any sign of anyone yet."

"I'm hanging on the phone while you get there. Watch your back and stay out of sight."

"I hear you."

Liam listened as North drove the truck around to the cabin.

"I'm here now. The dogs are happy to see me."

Liam could hear the truck door opening.

"Place looks the same. I'm walking inside. I guess I can't take a chance turning on lights either, can I?"

Liam faced Lilianna. "Do you ever leave lights on when you leave?"

She nodded. "I leave the outside porch light on and the kitchen light on."

He told North.

Liam could hear North as he walked to those lights and the gentle *click*s as he turned them on. "That gives me at least something to pack up by. Give me five. I'm putting the phone on the table, then going upstairs to get our gear."

There was a *clink* as the phone was set on the table. Liam listened to his footsteps as he raced up the stairs.

He hadn't unpacked and neither had North. But they

had the time line posted up on the wall. Liam figured it would take three minutes to get that down, another couple minutes to grab the bags.

Just as he was counting out those minutes, North's voice came through the phone. "Upstairs is clear. I'm taking this out to the truck." A minute later he came back in. "I'm clearing out the laptop and the paperwork we had in the living room and the kitchen. Taking that out to the truck now." Again he came back in the cabin. "Now I'm going to Lilianna's room."

Liam waited; Lilianna paced. She could hear everything North was saying as he worked his way through collecting the rest of the things from the house.

"What about the dogs?" Liam asked her.

Surprised, she asked, "Can he take them?"

North came back a few minutes later slightly out of breath. "Okay, I've got the gun, the money, the passport and paperwork, her electronics. Did either of you consider the dogs?"

"We definitely want to keep them safe," Liam said. "Maybe pack her a bag if you don't mind. I saw a couple in her room. I believe she does a lot of traveling." He turned to look at Lilianna.

Lilianna nodded. "Two suitcases are in the closet."

"On it." Suddenly North was back. "I've packed up what she needs."

"Load the dogs in the bed of the truck. And maybe take the truck down to the copse of trees behind the cabin. See if you can hide it there."

"Okay, back in the truck. Dogs are in the bed," North reported.

They listened as he turned on the truck engine and slowly drove toward the trees.

She said, "A road is along the back there, where we bring in feeding grain. There is a small shoulder area, for turning around. If he went down there, he should be able to park okay."

Giving instructions, they waited while North took the truck around the back.

He parked and hopped out. "Okay, I'm here with the dogs. The truck is safe. I've got the bulk of the material from Lilianna's place. I'm looking up, and I can see the cabin just on the side of the hill."

"Does everything look okay?" Lilianna asked.

"Yeah, so far so good," North said in a dry tone. "I'm about to spend the night out in the bush, watching."

"I don't think you'll have to wait long." Liam turned to Lilianna. "Go ahead and tell your sister you're in town for the evening. With both of us."

She studied him. "I sure hope you're wrong."

"So do I," he said.

She pulled out her phone and sent her sister a text.

Almost immediately she got an answer back. **About time you answered me.**

Lilianna shook her head. "Even over a text she can sound peevish."

"North, did you hear that? She's just been told we're gone from the cabin and will be for a while."

"Gotcha," North said. "I'll find a lookout spot with the dogs and see what we see."

Liam turned to look at Lilianna. "Would your sister hurt the dogs?"

She shook her head. "No, of course not. But the dogs also wouldn't stop her from going inside if she wanted to search my place for something."

"And, if the dogs weren't there, would she expect you to have them with you?"

She frowned and bit her lip as she thought about it. Then she shook her head. "No, I don't think so. I do take the dogs sometimes, but usually only when I'm around the property."

"So the fact that the dogs are gone would be a giveaway that something's up?"

She shrugged. "No, I don't think so. I have friends in town. I often go to their place. The dogs need socializing too, so I take them over to play with their dogs sometimes."

"Okay, North. All hands on deck. I don't know if you can get close enough to hear or close enough to take a video, but watch your back. I don't trust anybody on that property right now."

North laughed. "Don't you worry. You know as well as I do, there are not many people I trust anywhere in the world. Over and out." And North hung up.

Chapter 6

T HE NIGHT PASSED slowly. Nobody came to visit her dad. Her father never woke. She woke up herself several times to find she'd passed out on the couch from exhaustion. At one point Liam sat with his back against a wall, his eyes closed. But he appeared to be completely happy where he was. At another point, he told her, "Go back to sleep."

He hadn't even opened his eyes. She decided she wouldn't argue. She lay back down on the couch, closed her eyes and fell asleep again. But it seemed like she only slept for a few minutes, then she was awake all over again.

When she checked her watch the next time, it was ten to six. There was no sign of Liam. She sat up, groggy, grabbed her phone to see if anything was happening, but there wasn't even another text from her sister. As there was no sign of Liam, she wasn't sure what was going on. She got up, used the bathroom, washed her face, came out to check on her father and found he was asleep still, but it was a worrisome sleep as he hadn't changed position at all. She checked his neck with two fingers and found a strong, steady pulse.

As she went to sit on the couch, the door opened, and Liam walked in carrying two coffee cups. Her face lit up as she saw the coffee. "Where have you been?"

He smiled as he sat beside her and handed her a cup. "The cafeteria opened at six, so I figured I would see if I could be the first on the fresh pot."

She laughed. "Thanks, I need this."

"You do. More than you know. I have bad news for you."

She slowly placed the cup on the coffee table and turned to face him. "What?"

Liam settled on the couch.

"What do you mean, *bad news?*" she repeated.

His lips quirked at her hard tone. "Your cabin had a visitor last night."

She stared at him. "My sister?"

He shook his head. "No. A man."

"What man?" she asked, her voice harsh.

"I'm not sure, but I'll hazard a guess it was Carlos."

She shook her head. "Why? What could they possibly want from my place?"

"We don't know if there was a *we* involved," he said. "What we do know, of course, is that a single man went in."

"Did North see him?"

"He watched as a single male approached the cabin. He kept the dogs in the hollow, out of the way. He didn't want the dogs to bark and to give away where he was."

"The dogs are pretty laid back around Carlos. He spent enough time at my place," she said. "So it's no wonder they wouldn't have caused a ruckus. They wouldn't have if it had been Brianna either."

Liam nodded. "That's what we figured."

"Did North figure out what he was after?"

He shook his head. "North stayed in the copse of trees. But the lights went on all around, including the upstairs."

"So he was searching for something."

Liam nodded. "Any idea what?"

"No, not really," she said. "I had a little bit of money and my documentation, which I intended to put into a safe-deposit box and never got around to it."

"If you travel a lot, maybe you need the passport?" he guessed.

"Most of my travels have been domestic," she said. "But that could change at any time. I guess it was just the convenience of knowing I didn't have to make an extra trip for it."

"Most of us keep our passports at home," he said, "unless you don't travel at all. Then maybe it makes sense. What other documentation did you ask him to pick up?"

"Birth certificates, pictures of my brother, documentation for my father, title of the land, things like that. Most of it could be gotten from copies the lawyer is holding, but, since I'm not talking to the lawyer anymore …"

Liam chuckled. "You were pretty quick to fire him."

"Yep, as soon as I heard he was trying to pull a fast one," she said darkly. She glanced at his phone. "Any communication with doctors or lawyers yet?"

"The lawyer should be contacting you directly," Liam said, his tone easy and comforting. "Still waiting for the business day to start for the doctors."

She frowned, turned the coffee cup around in her hand as if pondering something.

"What's bothering you?" he asked.

She snorted. "What's not bothering me? There's just so much wrong."

Just then they heard a series of enduring sniffles and light snorts coming from the bed. Lilianna hopped to her feet and rushed to her father. Liam joined her at the end of the bed.

There was a little more color in her father's face, a little more life to his movements. Her father rolled to his back and opened his eyes. He gave a sigh as if not happy with what he saw.

"Father?"

Jim turned to look at her. He smiled. "Brianna."

She stepped forward and, with a misty smile, said, "No, Dad, it's Lilianna."

He frowned, searched her gaze, then lay back down on the bed, reaching up to rub his face. "I never could tell you apart." He looked over at Lilianna, his eyebrows raised.

She shrugged. "You used to be pretty good at it, Dad. You always said there was such a fundamental difference between us that it was pretty easy to tell us apart."

He frowned at her. "That was before," he said briskly. "I don't think it was recent."

She didn't argue with him, just patted his hand. "How was your night?"

He looked around, but a confused look was in his eyes. "Fine." He half sat up on the bed. "Why are you here?"

"You don't remember us coming last night?" she asked softly.

Her father frowned. He looked from her to Liam, and his frown deepened. "Who are you?"

"A friend of Gunner's," Liam said gently but fast enough that he cut off Lilianna's answer.

Jim's face eased back. He nodded. "Good man."

Lilianna was overjoyed her father was talking. He was closer to what he'd been months ago.

There was still some confusion, but he was throwing it off rather well. He sat up, tossed back the bedcover and said, "You shouldn't be here this early. I'm not even dressed."

"For the last few weeks, maybe longer, Dad, they haven't

bothered dressing you at all."

He sat and stared at her. "Who is *they?*"

She sent a worried glance to Liam, and he put an arm around her shoulders.

"You're still in the same assisted-care home," Lilianna said quietly. It broke her heart to see the fear and confusion in the man's eyes as he glanced around.

"How long have I been like this?" he asked. He reached out a hand, but it was trembling.

Liam stepped forward. "Quite a while. You had an argument with a nurse several months back. After that they gave you medication to calm you down and make you easier to get along with."

He closed his eyes and sat there for a long moment.

Liam asked, his voice low, "Do you want to walk to the bathroom yourself or do you want a hand?"

Lilianna's father's eyes opened up. There was still confusion and a lack of trust. But they settled on Liam. "How do you know Gunner?"

"I work for Levi. Logan works with me."

Her father's shoulders sagged. He reached up a hand; Liam gently pulled him to his feet and supported him as he walked over to the bathroom. He went into the bathroom and shut the door.

Liam turned to look at Lilianna, seeing the dismay on her face. "You should be happy. He appears to be throwing off the drugs faster than we expected."

She stared at Liam. "If he's like this now, would he have been like this the last four months?"

He shrugged. "I don't know for sure, but I'd say yes."

She clapped a hand over her mouth. "The difference is night and day. He's a very willful man. That's why it was so damn hard to see him go down the way he did. Yet I understood. We lost Keith too," she said tearfully. "But it was so hard to watch Dad give up like that."

"I wonder how much he gave up on his own and how much other people helped him," Liam said in a dark tone.

She cast him a sideways glance. "I don't like what you're implying."

"You haven't liked anything I've had to say in the last twenty-four hours. That doesn't mean I'm wrong to say it."

She winced. "No, you're right. I do need to hear it, and we do need to get to the bottom of this. But, so far, all you've said is that my brother-in-law went into my cabin and searched it. Well, potentially my brother-in-law. There are other men on the place."

"Exactly."

She pulled the hair tie from her hair, letting waves of long dark hair hang down; then she ran her fingers through it as she sat down on the edge of her father's bed. "I need a shower, a change of clothes and some answers," she said determinedly. She glanced out the window. "Where is North?"

"Standing watch at the cabin still."

"Why bother now?" she asked. "Somebody has already been there. Surely not more than one person would search it."

"I can't be sure of that. Would anybody else know you weren't there? Could your sister have told someone else?"

She shrugged. "My sister could've told someone, and, of course, anybody who works here in the home could have seen both of us here."

He nodded. "I talked to Katie. She said that generally this place has no problems. It's considered to have a very high quality of care."

Lilianna nodded. "Which is why I trusted them with my father," she said sadly. "Maybe I shouldn't have."

"Let's just say, it's a good thing that we're doing what we're doing now."

Just then the bathroom door opened, and her father stood there a little taller, yet still shaky. Liam walked over and gave an arm for him to use to get to the bed. Jim hesitated. Lilianna held her breath. But then he took hold of Liam's rock-solid arm and allowed himself to be helped to the bed.

As soon as he sat down again, Lilianna said, "Do you want to stay in bed or do you want to get dressed?"

Her father looked at her. "I want you to tell me what the hell's going on."

Even Liam appeared startled to hear the strength in Jim's voice. Maybe he was finally waking up from the stupor he'd been in for the last couple years.

"What's the last thing you remember?" she asked.

He shrugged. "Things I don't want to remember. Lots of it's just a dream state. Lots of it's just mixed up."

"You remember Keith?"

He glanced at her and gave a sad nod. "I do."

"Good, then we don't have to go through that again," she said quietly. "Do you remember walking away from life because of Keith?"

He stared at her, and his eyebrows rose. "What do you mean, *walking away from life*?"

"You were so despondent that you basically became so depressed and so locked inside of yourself that nobody could talk to you. You wouldn't do anything. You wouldn't look after yourself. You wouldn't eat. You barely got dressed or left the house anymore."

Liam watched Lilianna's dad's lower lip tremble.

"It wasn't that bad, was it?" he asked, clearly hoping for a different answer than what he saw in her face.

"It was worse," she said firmly. "I did everything I could to bring you back. But, as far as you were concerned, without your son, there was no reason to live anymore."

Lilianna felt her heart break. There was as much joy as sadness racing through her. All of a sudden her father was back the way he had been. She squatted in front of him. "I need you back," she cried out. "I need you back to being a normal living, happy human being. Not the shell of a man you were before you were brought here."

He looked around the room. "I have to admit," he said quietly, "I don't remember a whole lot."

"When you stopped looking after yourself, you were brought here for treatment, but, instead of getting better, you got worse. Four months ago, you attacked a nurse, and they drugged you to make sure you were more amiable to being looked after. But Keith ..." She took deep breath. "He died two years ago."

Her father stared at her, the color bleaching from his face. He shook his head. "No. No. No."

She grasped his fingers firmly and said, "Yes. And that's enough now. I need you back."

He lay down as if the shock was too much.

She pulled the covers over him. "It'll take a little while for the drugs to completely leave your system. I sent all your medical records to another specialist. But I'm damn glad to hear you speak and that you recognize me."

"Prove that you're Lilianna," he said, his voice weak.

She froze and looked down at him. "How do I prove

that?"

He stared at her, but something in the back of his gaze made her wonder. She leaned forward. "I'm the quiet one. I'm the one who always stood behind a little. Brianna and Mom do whatever they want. You weren't even at the wedding."

"What wedding?"

"Carlos married Brianna."

He stared at her, his head shaking almost in fear now. "No. He was supposed to marry you."

"He was supposed to, yes," she said. "But then Brianna slept with him. … After that, apparently he preferred her." She told the news in a matter-of-fact way, but inside she knew it wasn't a matter of *fact*. There was just so much pain. That simple betrayal had clearly annihilated her self-confidence. Up until she'd found them in bed, she'd been positive Carlos had loved her and only her.

She'd been completely taken in. She had wanted to believe Carlos had made the switch out of love, but now she wondered. The question now was, why had he gone to her cabin? What was he after? She didn't have anything special, and she certainly didn't have anything valuable. They had more than she had.

She straightened and looked at her father. "Do you believe me?"

His eyes closed. He nodded his head. "I need to sleep," he said faintly. "I need rest."

She looked at Liam, a question in her gaze.

He nodded and stepped forward. "Go ahead and rest. We will talk to the doctors."

Her father's eyes popped open, and he glared at Liam. "Sounds like people should have been talking to the doctors all along."

Lilianna felt a stab a guilt. "I did," she snapped back. "Look. This isn't the time to argue about that. I'm just glad to have you a little more cognizant and aware of your surroundings."

A heavy sigh heaved out of her father's chest, and he seemed to cave in on himself. "I'm sorry," he whispered. "It's a little hard to realize you've lost a couple years of your life."

"Even harder for those who watched you willfully step away," Liam said, his voice curt.

A whisper of pain crossed her father's face.

She shook her head. "Handing out blame won't help anybody. But I want to make sure you aren't given any more drugs."

Her father rolled to his back. "Is that likely?"

"I'm not sure," she said. "We've put an awful lot of legal stuff in play now to stop more of that from happening."

"You were supposed to have power of attorney," he said. "You knew that."

"I only have POA over your medical needs. Nothing else."

Her father turned to her. "What the hell's happened in the last couple years?"

"I'm not sure," she said. "I contacted Gunner for help because it seemed like the sanctuary was being attacked, our name besmirched, all the charity funds were drying up. But when Liam and North arrived, they cut to the chase and saw right to the bigger problems. And that is, your medication had been changed without my knowledge, and what I thought was a natural decline in your condition—this according to your doctors—was actually them drugging you," she said boldly. "And then we found out Brianna has been trying to set up power of attorney behind my back for control of your estate."

Alarmed, her father struggled to sit up in the bed. "No. I would never have given her that."

"Why not?" Liam asked.

He turned to look at Liam. "Do you know Brianna?" Jim challenged.

Liam shook his head. "No, I've only met her once."

"She's my daughter, and I love her dearly, but that doesn't mean I have to like who she is as a person. Most of the time she's fine. But once she gets close to her mother, things go bad."

"I haven't seen Mom in months," Lilianna said quietly. "I don't think she's part of the issue."

Jim snorted. "Better not be. I told that woman she'd never get her hands on my sanctuary."

"And yet that could be what's going on," Liam said into the sudden silence.

Lilianna wasn't sure what Liam was up to, but surely this much confusion and stress wasn't good for her father. She patted her father's hand. "You need to stay calm and focus on getting better."

He smiled. "Sounds like I need to focus on getting back on my feet."

Her face lit up in delight. "Yes, please."

He leaned forward. "And my elephants?"

She grinned. "All five are doing just fine. I still have the dogs, so that is at least normal." And then she remembered his house. "More or less, that is." She winced.

He stared at her. "What don't I know yet?"

"After Brianna and Carlos married, they moved into the main house."

He raised an eyebrow. "My house? And you?"

"I didn't want to live in the same house with them," she snapped. "I moved into the old worker's cabin."

"Where's my stuff then?"

She exchanged a look with Liam and looked back at her father. "I'm not sure. I haven't been welcome in the main house since."

His gaze narrowed. "I know I'm still weak, and I'm certainly not back in fighting form, but I want to have a talk with my lawyer and doctor. I want to get discharged."

"You have to understand the argument for the POA is that you're not of sound mind to handle your own business affairs." Liam filled in some of what they had found out so far. "With the change in the medications, sir, that made it easy to push this through. They did have to wait a reasonable time for medications to be changed and for doctors to make a final diagnosis."

"What time is it?" her father asked.

Liam looked at his watch. "It's seven-thirty."

Her father sighed. "So still too early to call anyone?"

"If you're trying to call the lawyer, I should tell you that I fired him last night." Lilianna's voice was calm, low but hard. "He didn't tell me about Brianna's attempt at getting power of attorney."

Her father stared at her in growing alarm. "But if our lawyer is not on our side ..."

"Exactly. But you've missed a lot in two years," she said. "You need to take some time to get caught back up."

"What lawyer have we got now then?"

"Gunner's lawyer," Liam said. "And I expect all hell to break lose any minute."

He frowned at Liam, his mind obviously processing if

that was a good thing or a bad thing.

Just then the door opened. Lilianna turned and watched as her sister walked in the door.

Brianna stopped in the doorway, turned and slammed the door closed behind her. "Just what are you doing here?" she snapped at Lilianna.

Lilianna raised an eyebrow. "I stopped in to see Dad. Why? When were you here last?"

"I'm here a lot," she said stiffly.

Lilianna turned her head to the side. "Really? I'm not so sure about that."

But her sister glared at her. She looked over at Liam and snorted. "What the hell is he doing here?"

Liam gave her a brief smile. "I have every right to be here. What are you doing here?"

The question stopped Brianna midstride. "What's going on?"

But it was her father who spoke up. "That's a good question, Brianna. Why is it you're trying to exert power of attorney over me?"

She turned to stare at him, and her jaw dropped. "You're awake?"

"Not only am I awake," he snapped, "but I'm pissing mad."

LIAM GRINNED. IF there was one thing he was glad to have seen, it was Brianna's wind taken out of her sails. She shoved her hands in her jeans pockets as she studied him. "When did this happen?"

"Not soon enough." Jim glared at his daughter. "Are you responsible for the drug that kept me docile?"

She stared at him. "We didn't have any choice," she said, her voice supergentle. "Let's not forget you attacked a nurse."

"Says who?" Lilianna challenged. "As if he'd attack anyone."

"I have to wonder about that too," her father said. "I'll be waiting to hear the full report on that incident."

Brianna shrugged as if it had nothing to do with her. "I'm sure there's paperwork somewhere," she said airily. She glared at Lilianna. "I want to visit with my father alone," she said stiffly.

"Too bad," Lilianna said cheerfully. "We're here. We'll be here all day."

Brianna stared at her. "Why?"

"To make sure nobody else drugs him, at least for the moment." Lilianna gave her a big smile. "And, of course, we have a lot of legal documentation to deal with."

"What are you talking about?" Brianna's voice became irritable.

"Well, I have always had power of attorney." Lilianna's smile gentled. "But somebody tried to pull a fast one."

Brianna stared at her, her bottom lip trembling. She firmed it up, and her nose rose several inches. "I don't have a clue what you're talking about. Of course you have POA over Dad's medical care. So?" She studied her sister, her chin rising higher. "Besides, it's not like you'd have the guts to do what needed to be done."

"That's not true," Lilianna cried out. "I've always done what's right. Unlike you."

"You're still holding Carlos against me, aren't you?" It was said with a dramatic waving of her hands.

Lilianna snorted. "He's an asshat. And you're welcome to him." She gave a dismissive wave of her hand.

But, if anything, that just made Brianna's back go up. "You will not speak about my husband that way."

"Well, as he's my ex-fiancé, I'll speak about him any way I want." Lilianna stood, drawing herself up to her full height.

Liam was surprised. He had yet to see that side of Lilianna. Maybe it was a good thing. He wasn't sure where it was coming from, but, if there was ever a time to find a backbone, it was right now and over the next twenty-four hours. Because there would be shit hitting the fan.

Brianna said, "I know it was a terrible shock for you, such a major rejection to realize he never did love you."

"I understood a long time ago that Carlos doesn't love anyone. So he doesn't love you either. You just haven't seen the light yet." Lilianna now had a saccharine smile. "And, if you think you'll pull any fast ones over on me and try to take the place away from Dad, you've got another think coming."

And that seemed to shock Brianna. Liam studied her face intently. He also had his cell phone on Record, in case anybody said anything of interest.

Brianna took several steps away, looked at her father and said, "I'll come back and visit you later." She turned and walked out.

Liam said, "Stay here with your father. I'll follow her outside."

Lilianna nodded, but he could see her bravado was already waning. She sagged onto the bed beside her father, who reached out a hand and grabbed her fingers.

"Thank you for being my champion," he said softly.

She shook her head. "Don't thank me. Apparently I did a shitty job."

"That's the trouble with being innocent," he said. "We aren't prepared for the wolves in the world."

THAT WAS THE last Liam heard as he walked out of the room and down the hall. He could see Brianna ahead, strutting forward, her voice loud and strident as she spoke on the phone.

"She knows something about the paperwork and the property. And the nurse situation. No, I don't know how she knows. We need to get it resolved now."

He raced behind her, and, as she stepped through the front doors, he stepped in front of her and smiled. "The cops want to speak with you by the way."

She froze when she heard his words, shrieked and dropped her phone. He put his foot on top of it. She stared at him, glanced at the phone, and he smiled.

"You're not going anywhere. And you're certainly not meeting dearly beloved Carlos, who's trying to push the paperwork through for you." He bent down and snatched up her phone, keeping it away from her. He checked the number. "Interesting." He lifted the phone and said, "Hello?"

A man's voice said, "Who's this?"

"The man who'll take you down," Liam said. He hit End Call. Instead of giving her the phone back, he pocketed it. "We need that for evidence." He grabbed her by the arm. "Let's go sit on a bench."

She shrugged his hand off, speaking furiously. "Unless you're a cop, you let me go right now."

He pulled out his own phone and said, "You'll stay here on a citizen's arrest until the cops do arrive." Levi answered his call immediately. "I have Brianna here. She's been caught on her phone trying to push paperwork through now that Lilianna's father is awake."

"He's my father too, damn you," Brianna cried out.

"I've told her the cops want to talk to her, and she's being difficult," Liam said in a mild tone.

"Not a problem," Levi said. "She stays right where she is in front of you. North is on his way, as is Detective Olson."

"How do I know that name?"

"He's the man who investigated Lilianna's brother's death." There was silence for a long moment, then Levi said, "ETA for both of them is ten minutes and five minutes, respectively."

"As long as you are sure Detective Olson is clear, that he's not taking a bribe in regard to her brother and his accident. I also have confiscated her phone. I'm sure a shit ton of damaging evidence is on that."

In front of him, Brianna shouted, "Give me my phone back, you thief."

"Is that her?" Levi asked, his tone calm.

"Oh, yeah. She's just a mouthpiece. Uses people like she uses shoes. Just to walk on."

Brianna stopped, cold, stock-still. "I do not." Once again, her nose went up. "My lawyers will hear about this."

"I'll be interested to see what lawyer you end up with."

She looked through a narrowed gaze. "Why? What do you know?"

He laughed. "A hell of a lot more than you do, sister."

Just then a police car flew into the parking lot. A middle-aged man hopped out.

Liam called out, "Detective Olson?" The man turned his head and nodded. "I'm talking to Levi right now. I'm Liam O'Brien."

Olson shook his hand, turned to look at Brianna and said, "I remember you. It was your brother's death I investigated."

Brianna nodded. She flicked Liam's shirt and said, "This man has accosted me. He's stolen my phone, and he's threatening me."

Detective Olson raised his eyes at Liam.

"Citizen's arrest. We believe she's keeping her father medicated so she can get power of attorney over his estate, including the elephant sanctuary and all the land included within." Liam grinned. "I always wanted to say something like that." He nodded. "She's in cahoots with her husband, and the family lawyer has already been fired, but you can bet that'll get ugly too."

Olson rubbed his temple. "Does any of this have to do with her brother's death?"

Liam turned his head slightly. "I would not be at all surprised."

And then Brianna turned on the crocodile tears.

Liam shook his head. "Save them for somebody who gives a shit." He turned to look at the detective. "You got this?"

He nodded and turned to Brianna. "I'd like to take you back to the station for questioning."

"Of course I'll come. My lawyer will meet me there too."

He nodded. "That's fine. We'll keep you there until your lawyer arrives."

Liam handed over her phone to the detective. "You'll need this."

Detective Olson pocketed it.

She stared at him. "I really don't understand what the problem is."

"We'll explain down at the station." The detective opened the back door of the police car for her. She glared at him but slid in.

Liam said, "May I see that phone for a moment?"

"You can't have access to any information on it."

"Watch your back," Liam said in a low voice. "The other sister's place was searched last night illegally. We're pretty sure it was this woman's husband."

The detective sighed. "If there's one thing I absolutely detest, it's family squabbles." He got into the vehicle, turned on the engine, locked all the doors and then drove away.

Liam's phone rang, and North said, "I'm pulling into the place. Is that Lilianna I just saw getting in the police car?"

"No, that's Brianna," Liam said with a laugh. "I pulled a citizen's arrest. Levi had already told the detective to get here fast because shit was coming down. He's taking her back for questioning. I caught her on the phone talking to somebody about pushing the paperwork through to make sure they got the sanctuary property locked up."

North whistled. "Wow. This has been a pretty fast open-and-shut case."

"Not so sure it's shut yet," Liam said. "On the other hand, the good news is that Lilianna's father has awakened and appears to be much more cognizant. He's also pretty damn pissed he's lost the last two years."

"I see you ahead."

Liam turned to see his truck driving toward him. He pocketed his phone and waited until North parked in front of him. He hopped out and pulled his phone from the dash. "How was last night?"

"Uncomfortable as hell. I took the floor. She had the couch, but, considering I was talking with you half the night, I figured neither one of us got much sleep." Liam shook his head. "What a business this is."

"What we still don't know though," North said as they walked toward Jim's room, "is if any of this has to do with the original reason she called us."

"It would have to though, wouldn't it?"

"On one hand it makes sense they would do something like that to slow the money down," North said. "But, on the other hand, if Brianna and her husband are living high on the hog with the charity's money, why would they cause it to dry up?"

"Unless they want the land for something else. Or part of the land," Liam suggested. He knocked on the door and turned the handle. As they stepped inside, he saw relief on Lilianna's face. "Did something happen?"

She shook her head. "Not necessarily but maybe. My new lawyer called. He wants to see me."

"That's probably a good idea. It's also a good idea to have the lawyers meet here. We'd get to the bottom of this sooner." He stepped forward. "The detective just took your sister in for questioning."

She stared at him. "What do you think my sister did beyond trying to get POA over the estate?"

"Don't know yet," he said. "But we need to find out, and fast."

She glanced at her father.

Liam followed her gaze to find her father curled up and sleeping. Liam nodded. "That's probably the best thing for him."

"Oh, I agree," North spoke up. "I have all your belongings here now too."

"Do you have any idea who went into my cabin?" she asked.

North shook his head. "I believe it was a male. But with a hoodie over his head, I couldn't tell you any more than that."

"And of course you couldn't get any closer, or the dogs would have given you away."

North nodded. "I tried to tie them down and leave, but they barked."

She winced. "I know. They hate being tied up." Her shoulders sagged. "Did you leave the dogs at the house?"

"Yes, left them in the yard. They appeared to consider that normal."

"It is. They are used to having the run of the place." She got up off her father's bed, walked to the couch and sat down. "If we at least had an answer as to who searched my home, I would know something for sure. But it seems like I don't know anything."

"Right now, we're building the investigation. We're deconstructing everything around us, pulling out all the half-truths, the known lies, trying to get to where the real skeleton of this issue is."

"Do you think there's more going on here than just my sister and Carlos?"

Liam nodded very slowly. "I think so, yes."

Chapter 7

S HE STARED AT him in horror. "How can there be? How is it possible there could be more shit like this?" She shook her head. "The only good thing is my father does appear to be returning to normal. But I don't know if he'll slide back again."

"Let's hope he doesn't. We should be hearing from the specialist soon."

Just then Liam's phone rang. She watched as he pulled it out, looked at her and said, "It's the specialist. Let me talk to him." He stepped out of the room.

"He could've talked to him in here," she said resentfully to North.

North grinned. "What he doesn't want is for your father to overhear."

Instantly she felt bad. "I'm not myself right now," she said with a weary sigh. "I need food. I need a shower and a change of clothes, and I need to get my life back on track."

"All of that is a good idea. Gunner is on his way."

She gave North a ghost of a smile. "That would be nice. Gunner has always been a good friend. He came here to visit my father a couple times, until he didn't even remember who Gunner was. It was very difficult for all of us."

"What we need to know is whether that was a case of his medication being increased or whether your father really was declining."

"It's too horrible," she said. "I feel so damn guilty already."

"You can only feel guilty about what you knew and what you could have actively changed," North said calmly. He sat down at the end of the couch and turned to face her. "If you beat yourself up over things you couldn't have changed, there's really no way to go forward."

She frowned at him. "Do you guys handle cases like this all the time?"

He chuckled. "I'm not sure many cases are like this. But cases where there's family doing shit to family? That happens way too much."

"Do you travel all over the world?"

"We're both relatively new in Levi's company. But Levi handles jobs all over the world, yes. From kidnappings and terrorist attempts to simple things like drug deals and getting caught up in shootings and kidnappings and sex trafficking."

Her mouth dropped open. "Sex trafficking?"

North nodded, giving her a grim smile. "There was a pretty ugly case in Boston. A nurse who was kidnapped by another person who worked at the same hospital. By the time Levi's team had cracked it open, there was quite a wealth of nastiness going on there."

She frowned. "Logan may have mentioned something about that." She shook her head. "Seems like he's talked to me about so many different things."

North nodded. "And of course there's always Flynn and Anna."

"I remember their case too." She sighed. "It's so horrible when people could do good, and instead they spend all their money and time for the wrong things."

"That's called humanity," North said.

Just then the door opened, and Liam walked back in.

She gave him a frown. "Next time have the conversation here where I can hear it, please."

"Not if that means your father hears it too." He grabbed a chair and plunked it down across from the couch. "The specialist has gone over the medical chart. I gave him an update, that your father had been lucid this morning. He wants to see him today. We'll run some blood tests. We don't really know if any criminal activity involves the assisted-care home or not. It could be just that this was their best guess for your father's care."

She shook her head. "No way in hell that was best."

"Maybe," Liam said gently. "But don't forget, these are doctors who only see their patients for a few minutes in a day. The condition that they present at that time often determines the next course of action."

"Are you excusing their analysis of my father's condition?"

He chuckled. "Hell no. I'm just happy to see you fighting for him."

She shook her head. "I was just telling North how guilty I feel about not having been there for him."

"What do you think you could have done?" Liam asked curiously.

She glared at him. "I don't know. But I should have seen his decline was really bad. It doesn't matter now. Go on—what else is happening?"

"The specialist is on his way. He will bring his nurse, and they'll take several vials of blood. He also wants to assess your father's condition now. As soon as he gets the blood tests back, then he'll go forward with the treatment plan."

"Do you think he'll still need anything?" she asked hopefully. "The fact that he was so lucid this morning makes me think he just needs rest."

"If that's the case, then there's a good chance your father can go home soon."

She lit up with joy, but, as the words settled, her heart sank. "And where does that mean?"

"Exactly," Liam said. "Will he be safe at home?"

She stared at him but understood what he meant. "I'd have said Brianna would never hurt him," she said slowly. "The problem is, I don't know who she is right now."

He nodded. "Think about that. And think about what she's done already."

"The trouble is, I don't know what she's done," she cried out.

"No, and, until the lawyers get together, there's no way to know the whole story—if then," he said. His phone rang again. He pulled it out. "Speaking of which, here's the new lawyer." He answered several questions before turning to Lilianna. "The lawyer wants to see your father's condition for himself."

"Tell him to come after the specialist," she said mutinously. She watched Liam laugh; then he passed on her message formally.

He glanced at his watch. "Sure, eleven is fine." He raised his gaze and his eyebrows at Lilianna. She nodded, and he ended the call. "Since we can't leave Jim alone or easily take him out, I guess this is where visitations take place."

She smiled and nodded. "I should be damn glad he's capable of having these conversations."

"True. But it'll also take him a few days. He's weak. He'll tire easily, and, if he's expecting to go home to the sanctuary and to traipse across the acres, that won't happen quickly."

She sighed. "I know."

Liam turned to North. "I don't know that the food here is any more edible than other hospital-like settings."

North chuckled. "I highly doubt it. I see you got a half cup of coffee sitting here." He stood. "Do I make the coffee and food run?"

Lilianna looked at him. "I hate to ask you …"

He shrugged. "I have to eat too. Your father can't be left alone. If he's coming back to himself, it'll put a major crimp in somebody else's plans." He walked out the door.

Lilianna turned and glanced at Liam. "Do you really think somebody would try to kill my father now?"

"Not initially. Not as long as the paperwork was being put into place," Liam said quietly. "But now …" He gave her a hard smile and added, "You could be in danger too."

His words were a blow to her stomach. She stared at him. "You've gone very quickly down the rabbit hole," she snapped. "I'm not in any danger."

"We'll see," he said. "How long have you known your old lawyer?"

She shrugged. "He's been my father's lawyer since forever." She stared off in the distance, trying to wrap her mind around dates. "Everything got a little fuzzy around the time of my brother's death," she admitted. "And I apparently lost my grasp on some of reality too. I let a lot of things slide."

"You can't keep thrashing yourself with guilt over that," he said. "There's more to life than taking the blame. If you were close to your brother, and you loved him, then his loss would have been huge for you."

"It was," she admitted "It was massive. At the same time,

it's not really an excuse, is it?"

"Do you need an excuse?"

She glared at him. "Why won't you let me feel bad?" she complained good-naturedly.

He chuckled. "It's not allowed. I'm in the camp that says things happen for a reason. We don't always know where or when or why, but it's not always up to us to ask those questions and to expect answers. We have to deal with the hand we've been dealt."

She nodded. "I get that. But how does one deal with the fact you didn't do as good a job as you could have?"

"Do better next time?" he asked, a grin on his face.

"Lord, I hope there isn't a next time," she muttered.

"What would you normally be doing today?"

"Going through paperwork. Touching base with charities, writing up several press releases and talking to a couple newspapers to see if I could get some good promo to rebuild our name."

"Can you do any of that from here?"

"If North leaves me my laptop, I should be able to."

"Good. Then plan on staying here for the day while we get your father, the lawyers and the doctors and whatnot squared away. And we'll get back to your cabin tonight."

"I'm trying to figure out who was at the cabin last night," she said. "Some of the staff members work directly with us. A couple men who live close by. Yet I can't see them having any reason to go into the cabin."

"Which is why it comes down to Carlos, because, of course, he also was the one who would have understood from the text messages that Brianna sent you, that you weren't home."

"I get that. Still, I can't see Carlos going through my

house," she exclaimed. "There's nothing there for him to take."

Liam thought for a long moment. "Maybe he wasn't there to *take* but was there to *place*."

She stared at him, completely confused as to what he was talking about. She leaned forward. "I know I need coffee, but it sounds like you need a shot of something much stronger," she joked.

He grinned. "And I wouldn't say no. I'm not Irish for nothing. But what if …" He stared off in space for a long moment. "What if he placed something in your cabin? Either something incriminating or something that would help him incriminate you."

"Incriminate me in what?" she exclaimed. "That makes no sense."

"Maybe he set up bugs in your cabin," Liam said gently. "So then he could track all the conversations you had while we were there."

She frowned. "You mean, like listening devices? Like supersecret spy stuff?"

His grin flashed, and she realized she'd do an awful lot to keep that smile flashing in her direction. She didn't know what was so special about him, but something definitely made her heart jump up and down, but that wouldn't get her where she needed to go. Forcibly she brought her attention back to the subject matter. "How would I know?"

"We can search it when we get back."

She had visions of them flipping mattresses and checking inside cupboards. "I thought they were pretty small these days. How would we find them?"

"We have a device that can usually pick up any bugs."

She frowned, not liking that. "Do you think anybody's

trying to hurt the elephants?" she asked hesitantly. "Because I don't think I could handle it."

"Maybe as a finale, if it would result in you moving the animals someplace else. I don't know the life expectancy of elephants …"

"Decades," she said shortly. "The sanctuary needs to be financed for at least another forty to fifty years for those we have right now."

"And that reconfirms how we really need your father on his feet and back at the helm."

She sighed. "I hate waiting."

"It's not been very long yet."

She glared at him. "Speak for yourself. I've been waiting for my father to get back to normal for two years, and then I had to deal with this whole nightmare regarding the website and the deluge of bad press all of a sudden. It took me a long time to get to the point where I was talking to Gunner about it."

"I'm glad you did, and obviously it was the tipping point for all this."

In the distance she heard a gentle voice. She bounded to her feet and raced to her father. "Dad, are you awake?"

There was a sigh and one word, "Yes."

She smiled down at him, desperate to hold back the tears. "Do you know who I am?" she asked hesitantly.

He rolled to his back, reached up a hand and said, "Lilianna."

She lifted his hand to her lips and dropped a kiss on his knuckles. "I'm so glad to see you back again, Dad."

"I don't know that I want to be back. It sounds like hell has gone down in my absence." He opened his eyes and stared at her. "Please tell me it was all a bad dream."

She shook her head. "I'm not sure which part you think might have been a bad dream, but the fact that you've been out for two years is certainly not a dream. That's a very sad reality."

He stared moodily around the room, his gaze lighting on Liam. His eyes narrowed, and he stared at Liam for a long moment. "Logan, Levi, Gunner," he said, tripping the names together in a rough thought pattern.

Liam stood and nodded. "Correct."

Relief crossed her father's face. "And the conversation we just had a little bit ago?"

Liam placed his hand on Lilianna's shoulder. "The truth, every bit of it."

Her father stared at the ceiling. "Now I feel old," he whispered. "Tired and old."

"No time for that," Liam said quietly. "There's a hell of a mess, and you need to be alert and aware of what's happening."

"You're Liam." Her father's gaze sharpened as he looked at him. "Explain?"

Instead, Lilianna gave him the rundown of the lawyers and doctors upcoming visits. "It's really important you are as alert as you can be," she said. "I don't know what's happening with the paperwork, but they've taken Brianna down to the station for questioning."

A shadow crossed her father's face. He stared at the blankets for a long moment and then sighed. "I love her dearly. But she's very much like her mother."

At that, Lilianna couldn't argue. There was a knock on the door, and she turned to see North coming in with bags in his hands.

He placed them on the small coffee table and shut the

door. He looked down at the older man, reached out a hand, shook it and said, "I'm North, another one of Levi's employees."

Her father stared at him for a long moment. "Two of you?"

"Two of us," North confirmed.

"Then it's bad, isn't it?"

"Bad enough. And, if you don't take your place as the head of the family and as the manager of the sanctuary," Liam said, "there's a good chance it won't be a sanctuary any longer."

The shock hit her father between the eyes. He brushed it away. "I don't know what you just brought in here, but it smells like food. I don't think I can handle eating right now. But I sure as hell won't face a battle without being showered, shaved and dressed."

"Do you want help?" Liam asked.

Her father pushed back his sheets, sat up and carefully stood. He considered the room for a moment. "It's not spinning. I'll take that as a good sign." And he marched slowly like an old solider toward the bathroom.

LIAM SMILED. HE liked the man's guts. He squeezed Lilianna's shoulders gently and said, "Come on. Let's get you some food. Leave your father to do what your father needs to do to get back to the world."

She stared at the bathroom door. "He looked much better, didn't he?"

Liam could hear the hope in her voice and nodded. "He did. More than that, he appears to understand what's going on around him."

"But he'll be off on dates and probably names," North said. "So, when he comes back out, we should talk about that, fill him in a bit."

Liam walked over to the bags while North explained to Lilianna how sometimes the drugs left pockets of memories empty. Liam opened the bags, smiled and brought out several big sealed containers.

"What all did you get?"

"Everything but the kitchen sink. I wasn't sure how long we'd be here, and I wasn't sure if your father was eating," he said apologetically to Lilianna. "I was hoping he would, but I think he's right. His stomach will be a little on the touchy side."

"But he's been eating steadily," she said, "maybe not a lot though. I don't know how the withdrawal of the drugs will affect him."

"We'll ask him when he comes out," Liam said firmly. He pointed to the corner of the couch and said, "Sit."

She shot him a look and sat down. "You know I'm not a dog, right?"

He chuckled. "At least not a well-trained one."

She snatched up a napkin, wadded it in a ball and chucked it at him.

He laughed out loud.

North said, "Children, children." He brought out paper plates and plastic knives and forks. "I suggest we dig into this before the shit hits the fan."

Liam opened the containers to find stacks of pancakes, a container of scrambled eggs and another one of sausages. In still another tin-foil-wrapped package, there was toast. He shook his head. "I have no idea where you got all this, but it looks delicious."

"Anything looks delicious when you haven't eaten in twelve hours, and you got no sleep to boot," North said calmly. He took two sausages, two pancakes and scooped up some eggs, then grabbed a piece of toast. "Eat up." He sat back down on the couch.

As if galvanized by his words, Lilianna grabbed her plate and served herself about half of what North had taken.

That was good because Liam had no intention of starving today. He served himself an equal portion to what North had and that left pretty close to what Lilianna had for her father, if he wanted any.

Liam hoped they'd have fifteen or twenty minutes to eat their meal in peace and to coach her father before they were interrupted. But he also knew a lot was going on today.

He'd just finished his pancakes and sausages, was starting on this toast with the eggs on top, when his phone rang. He sighed, placed his food on the table and pulled out his cell. He didn't recognize the number. "Liam O'Brien."

"This is Detective Olson."

Liam sat back. "Detective, what can I do for you?"

"I just spoke to Levi and filled him in on the details. I don't have any proof Brianna was involved in anything untoward at the property. There are lots of emails between her and a lawyer, and her and her husband, regarding paperwork and legal documents. I presume from what you're saying that Lilianna didn't know anything about this. Is that correct?"

"We're not sure what legal paperwork has been drafted," Liam said carefully. "Can you confirm the lawyer's name?"

"Eric Fulton," Detective Olson said.

Liam nodded. "That's the same lawyer."

"I don't have anything to charge her with at this point."

"No, I can see that," Liam said. "How long can you hold her?"

"The same Eric Fulton is here trying to get her released."

"Interesting. Can you hold her a little longer? Let me see if I can get the new lawyer there and see what's up?" He ended the call and made another. "Gunner, we got a problem."

After Liam explained, Gunner said, "I'll take care of it." And he hung up.

Liam slowly put his phone down. "So the lawyers may not be meeting because Fulton is trying to get the police to release your sister."

"She hasn't been charged with anything?" North asked.

Liam shook his head. "Not even sure right now what she would be charged with," he admitted.

"But Eric isn't a criminal lawyer," Lilianna protested.

Just then her father walked out of the bathroom. He looked a little shaky but also like a changed man. He stopped in front of the group, studied the food and said, "What's this about Eric?"

"He's the one trying to get Brianna released."

Her father raised his gaze. "Any chance I can go to the police station and see him there?"

Liam contemplated the advisability of that. "Not likely. But it depends on the doctors, but you definitely do need to see him. We'll see if he can come here."

Her father sighed, turned to look around the room. He was still pale, still a little shaky but said, "Where the hell are my clothes?"

Liam was afraid there weren't any. He glanced at Lilianna. "Do you want to track down some for him?"

She stood. "I'll talk to the nurses at reception." And she

disappeared out the door.

Her father sat in her place and studied the food. He grabbed a piece of toast and said, "This might sit." He slowly nibbled away.

"How much do you remember, sir?"

"I remember a huge chasm of black overwhelming grief that swallowed me up, sucked me dry. I couldn't get out of it—no how, no way," he said tiredly. "It's like nothing else mattered."

"I get that. Do you remember attacking the nurse?"

He shook his head. "I can't imagine that's something I would have done. It's not in my nature."

"There could have been a provoking incident," North said. "We need to find out what nurse was supposedly attacked, and what proof they have of the attack."

Her father sighed. "Eric is a friend. Why would he do this?"

"I don't know," Liam said. "The problem is, we don't know what anybody's doing."

North said, "Do you remember dates, names of the doctors? They'll need to know what level of acuity you have now."

Jim looked at him. "I remember your name is North, and his is Liam. I remember Eric was my lawyer, and I remember Gunner as being a good friend. I don't remember how so much time went by without my permission though." He started to get angry. "I don't remember hitting the nurse, and I don't remember very much about the last two years. There are bits and pieces moving in and out of a fog. And that's about it."

The men nodded. "If you can get that piece of toast down," North said, "maybe try for some protein as well."

Jim nodded. He extended his hand, staring at it. "I feel like I've lost fifty pounds and aged fifty years."

"You've been eating regularly," Liam said. "But your body has lost the vitality and vibrancy that comes with living an active lifestyle. You've been sitting on the couch or lying in bed for the bulk of the last couple years."

Her father shook his said. "I hated TV to begin with. I can't imagine how I got relegated to this."

"The question now is, whether you're capable of getting yourself back out of it."

"What battle is it you guys are here to fight?" Jim asked.

The men exchanged a look.

Jim shook his head. "None of that. I can't fight if I don't know who I'm up against."

Liam explained how Lilianna had gone to Gunner because she was afraid somebody was trying to defame the charity. He ended with, "The funds have dried up. And all kinds of rumors have talked of mismanagement of funds and poor treatment of the elephants."

Jim was aghast. "Anybody who knows me realizes how much I love those elephants."

Liam nodded and added, "But everybody understands you haven't been at the helm for the last two years. Everybody knows you loved your son so much that the blow of his death was crippling."

"So why now?" Jim stared off in the distance. "I've no doubt I can contact the charities again, tell them I'm back to health, or at least recovering," he corrected. "And get the money flowing again. We must have it for the elephants."

"I asked Lilianna what would happen if there wasn't money," Liam said. "And she said that, if worse came to worst, she would have to sell property."

With clear eyes, Jim looked at him. "That will never happen while I'm living and breathing."

"You didn't leave your daughter a whole lot of choice," Liam said. "You do realize her own personal money helps to keep you here?"

And once again it was like all the stuffing had drained out of him. He just sat there, tired and upset, trying to figure out what his world had come to. He shook his head. "That should never have happened."

"No, it shouldn't have. But medical care is expensive, and, when the insurance didn't cover everything required, she's the one who dipped into her savings."

Chapter 8

LILIANNA HOPED KATIE was at the front desk. She walked down the hallway, her mind churning and guilt eating her up. The trouble was, guilt wouldn't get her anywhere.

What she really needed was answers, and she needed them fast. The fact that her father was awake and appeared to be cognizant was an unbelievable miracle. It made her feel all the guiltier that he hadn't been this way for the last two years. She understood his initial problem had been grief, but would he have come out of that with some better medical assistance? Particularly in the last four months?

He was definitely struggling to throw off the effects of whatever it was he'd been under. And his body was weak. But inside she was so damn proud of him. He was awake; he did appear to be aware, and, if nothing else, he was back to being the father she hadn't seen in a long time.

Tears came to her eyes. She brushed them away as she walked up to the reception desk. She glanced around and said, "Is Katie still here?"

Katie peeked around the wall and smiled. "Lilianna, what can I do for you?" Then she cocked her head. "Are you crying? What's the matter?"

From the alarm in Katie's voice, Lilianna realized Katie thought something bad had happened. Lilianna gave her a watery smile. "Something very good. My father is much, much better. He's talking. He's cognizant. He knows who I am. He appears to be pulling out of whatever funk he was in."

Katie's face lit up. "Oh, my God! That's fantastic. I'm so happy for you."

Lilianna nodded. "He's gotten up, showered and shaved. And now we're looking for his clothes. He says he doesn't feel like himself wearing pajamas."

Katie nodded. "Isn't that the truth? It just seems to make us feel more invalid when we're in pajamas." She frowned. "But I'm not sure where his clothes are. Did you check his room?"

Lilianna shrugged. "I gave it a cursory look, but it's likely been a couple months since he dressed."

"Oh, dear. Well, all his personal belongings should be in a locker. Let me check in the back." She disappeared around the wall.

"I sure hope he's got something to wear," Lilianna muttered, her mind already racing, figuring out how she could get her father's clothing back. Because what she didn't know was what Brianna might have done with all her father's belongings in his house. Regarding her sister, Lilianna had this burning anger inside. That somebody could willfully do something to hurt her father, and be a family member, his own daughter, was just beyond comprehension.

Her mind ran out of options. There were only so many excuses she could make for Brianna. Lilianna didn't want to think Carlos was involved. But, then again, at one point she had trusted him with her body and her future. And he had betrayed both. How the hell was she supposed to deal with that? If he could do that, there was no end to the things he could do.

Just then Katie came back with a paper bag. She held it up and said, "This is all I have."

Her father's name and a date were written on the outside. It was from several months ago. Lilianna reached for the bag and opened it. "It appears to be pants and a shirt, so that might be enough to get us started. If you find anything else, let me know."

Katie nodded. "I'll leave a note for the girls. I was supposed to be off an hour ago, but my replacement hasn't shown up yet."

Lilianna nodded. "Oh, poor you. The night shifts are long enough without having to stay late."

"Sure enough," Katie said. "But it is what it is."

Lilianna turned, then realized just how many things had been wrong lately. "Who is supposed to replace you?"

"Maria," Katie said with a big smile. "She's been here for about six months."

"Is she good?" Lilianna asked. "But then I would presume so if she is on the day shift."

Katie chuckled. "She's very good, and it's awesome to have more staff. And, since Maria speaks Spanish, that's another huge help. In a place like this, having as many languages spoken here as we can get is the best. Of course ..." She frowned, then leaned forward. "She's the nurse who put in the complaint about your father."

"Is she? Now I really want to speak with her." Filing away that tidbit, Lilianna headed toward her father's room. She knocked on the door and pushed it open. Her father was on the bed with his eyes closed. She rushed forward. "You're doing too much too fast," she scolded.

He smiled and waved her off. "I'm fine. What did you

find?"

She held up a paper bag. "This is what they had."

He sat up slowly, looking at the bag with interest. "Let's see what's in there."

She took out a pair of pants and a shirt and a golf tee. The pants were a khaki brand he used to favor.

He looked at them and smiled. "Well, that's a really good start." There was a pair of underwear and socks. "At the bottom are my shoes. I was hoping those were inside with the weight."

"Right." She looked at him. "Do you want to get changed now? Or wait?"

Liam looked at her, but the look in his eye said that even one more decision was just too much for him.

She frowned. "You'll feel better if you dress."

Her father nodded and straightened, looking at the clothing. "I shouldn't be this tired."

"I imagine that the withdrawal of the drugs will make you off for several days," Liam said. "Just take it easy. We'll have quite the morning, and we need to make sure everything is handled properly."

Her father nodded. He struggled to his feet, grabbed the paper bag and went to the bathroom.

Lilianna looked at Liam. "Is he okay, do you think?"

Liam nodded. "He's a hell of a lot better than he was just hours earlier."

"I'd like to see a little more fire and vinegar. But it seems to come and go in small spurts, as if the energy is just too hard to keep up at that level." Lilianna sat on the couch beside Liam. "Katie is still here. Maria, the nurse my father supposedly attacked, didn't show up to work today."

Liam raised his gaze and looked at her.

Her lips twitched. "I was thinking the same thing. Do you think it's coincidental?"

"Hell no. Any idea why she didn't come?" Liam asked.

Lilianna shook her head. "I have no idea."

"We need to take a closer look at this." He nodded but pulled out his phone and jotted down something in a text.

"Do you send information as soon as you learn of it?"

"Absolutely. It's the only way to maintain any kind of understanding of what's happening. In this case I'm getting someone else to contact this missing nurse to see if she has anything to do with what's going on here."

Lilianna checked her watch. "It's nine o'clock. How long do you think we have to wait before somebody comes by?"

He shook his head. "Not long. I'm hoping to get your father dressed so he looks like a normal human being, not like a patient."

"As if patients aren't normal human beings?"

He grinned. "You know what I mean. First appearances and all that."

She nodded. "But, if I was him, I'd want to get the hell out of here."

"And that might happen too. It might also not be all that easy. I don't know what's required."

She sat back on the couch. "Where is North?"

"Gone looking for answers."

She stared at him, but he didn't offer anything else. She realized she wouldn't be let in on everything. "Do you think my sister is still at the police station?"

"No idea, but I imagine she'll be there until the police and lawyers hash this out."

"Do you think they'll both come here?"

"I highly suspect they're all coming here, including the

new lawyers and the old one," Liam said. "You'll need to defend your father from any onslaught coming his way."

She nodded. "I failed him these last few months. I won't fail him again."

"You can't look at it that way. You did the best you could with the information you had at hand. If you don't know how far somebody will go, you don't have a clue what they might do to achieve their goals."

"I never would have thought my sister would hurt my father."

"You don't know that she has. You don't know what her involvement is yet, so wait until we know for sure."

"Not so easy to do at this point. That she's trying to get POA over his estate makes me very suspicious."

"Me too. And, if something like this could happen to your father, it could also happen to you."

She stared at him in horror.

He shrugged. "No, I'm not saying that's what'll happen, but should it, they'd have sudden control over both estates."

"I don't have an estate," she said. "I don't have anything. Everything I've earned has gone to help my father."

He chuckled. "I know that. You know that. But we also know there are abuses happening all the time."

Her father opened the bathroom door and stepped out.

She looked at him in surprise. "Oh, wow! You look great," she said with joy.

He looked a little self-conscious and said, "They're a little big."

She gave him a kiss on the cheek. "You will fill them out fast enough," she teased.

He smiled. "I don't know about that." He looked at Liam. "At the moment I have some energy. Any idea when the lawyers are coming?"

Liam said, "It's hard to say now that Brianna was at the police station. Soon hopefully. But the specialist should arrive first."

Just then a knock was heard on the door and a man in a three-piece suit and an air of authority surrounding him walked in. He reached out a hand to Lilianna. "You must be Lilianna. I'm Dr. Splicer. Gunner sent me."

Her face lit up. "Thank you so much for coming," she said warmly. "This is my father, Jim Howell." She turned to her father, then back to the doctor. "You've seen his medical records?"

He nodded. "Medical records are helpful, but it's not the same as seeing the patient himself."

She watched as he studied her father.

"It's good to see you up and dressed," the doctor said directly to her father.

He nodded. "My daughter just found clothes for me. Apparently I've missed a couple years."

"And how do you feel about that?"

"Angry," was the snapped response.

"Good. Keep that anger firing. Let's give you a check over and see what we can find." The specialist faced Liam and Lilianna.

Liam said, "Do you want us to step outside?"

Both patient and doctor shook their heads.

The doctor nodded. "As long as it's okay with Jim."

Her father waved his hand. "Apparently she's been looking after me for the last couple years, so this won't make any difference."

The specialist nodded and said, "Then let's have you lay down and take a good look."

With Liam and Lilianna sitting on the couch watching, the doctor did a quick check and then asked Jim some questions. Like, what was his name, how old was he, when was he born. Things like that.

Lilianna listened intently. But she couldn't find anything in her father's voice that showed any confusion. She wanted to ask Liam if he'd coached her father, but Liam was sitting, relaxed, back on his phone. Completely unconcerned. She couldn't be so blasé. This was all about her father, and the chance of getting him back into her life in every way was tantalizingly close.

Finally the doctor stood straight and said, "My nurse is outside. He'll draw some blood. If possible, we'd like you to give us a urine sample." He looked at her father. "We'll get everything analyzed as fast as we can, but I don't see any reason for any medication at this point." He tapped the tablet in front of him. "I've gone over the treatment you've received to date, and, as far as I'm concerned, there is no need for the medications listed there any longer."

He held up a hand at Lilianna's delight.

"However, it'll take you a few days to get past the lingering effects of the drugs, not to mention the abrupt withdrawal from them. I don't want you left alone or unattended while you're withdrawing from these drugs. It's still possible you'll feel chills and the shakes. I don't want you falling accidentally."

Jim frowned. "I'd like to think that, at my age, I don't need anybody looking after me."

"But, as we already know, somebody has had to," the doctor said quietly. "Now that you're close to being back to normal, let's not slack off and have a bigger problem."

Lilianna jumped to her feet. "He can come home with

me," she said.

"I can go to my own home too," her father snapped. "Which means you can come home with me."

She nodded slowly. "There has been a lot of change in two years, Dad. We'll have to move forward gently."

"No, we don't. I just have to get back on my feet." He glared at the doctor. "How long do you think I need to be under watch?"

"A couple days. I would suggest you go to Gunner's place, make sure you're strong and steady on your feet again and that you're safe. I'm close by if there are any problems."

At the term *safe*, her father turned his gaze on Liam.

Liam shrugged. "If you want, you can stay in the cabin with us. Or, if you're up for the fight, we can clear out your home and put you back in as the head of the house." Liam took a step forward. "But, once you take that step, you need to make sure you remain in power and you can hold that position."

The specialist nodded. "Jim, you should listen to him. It sounds easy to step back into your old life. But others have moved on, and they aren't always happy to hand over the reins again. Particularly if assets are involved."

Her father lay back down again. "Maybe I'll go to Gunner's for a couple days, then see if I can get a few of his men to come with me and to ensure my house is returned to me in all forms."

"Before you do that," Liam said, "let's make sure we've got the lawyers on board."

Her father nodded and looked over at Lilianna. "Will you be safe?"

She didn't get a chance to answer. Liam jumped in. "I'll make sure she's safe."

A smile crossed her father's face. "Good to know. Good to know." He looked at the doctor. "When can we leave?"

The doctor walked back to the door, opened it and motioned for somebody to come in. "This is Jonah. Jonah, this is Jim. Jonah is my nurse. He travels with me when I have to do house calls."

"I don't imagine that's very often," Lilianna said.

The specialist shot her a look. "No, it isn't. This is a special favor for Gunner."

"I appreciate it," she said quietly. "When there are power plays in the works, you don't know who you can trust."

"I would already have said Gunner and Eric," her father said.

The nurse was setting up to take blood.

"Who is Eric?" the specialist asked.

"My lawyer. Or my ex-lawyer according to my daughter," her father said. "I really want to talk to that man."

"Maybe not just yet," the specialist said, watching as the nurse finished taking blood. "We do need to make sure you're strong enough to handle this added emotional and physical stress on your body."

Jonah gave her father a hand back onto his feet and handed him a clear plastic bottle.

Her father sighed and walked to the bathroom. "This is the not-so-nice part about tests," he muttered.

"Could be worse," Lilianna called out. "Just think of this as your ticket out of here."

The door closed with a hard snick.

She turned to the specialist. "Are you serious about not letting him talk to the lawyers? We're expecting them before noon."

"I'll have paperwork here to get your father released. If

Gunner's lawyer is coming too, that wouldn't be a bad idea, in case I run into any legal hassles. Who has power of attorney?"

"I do over his medical care, but my sister is trying to get power of attorney over his estate."

The specialist shook his head. "Like I said, gotta love families."

Just then the door opened again. The director stepped in and frowned. "Why is everybody in here? It isn't even visiting hours." His gaze zeroed in on the specialist. "And who are you?" he barked.

The doctor walked over, held out his hand and said, "I'm Dr. Splicer. I'm Jim's specialist."

The director shook his head. "He's in our care."

"Then you haven't checked your email this morning," Dr. Splicer said. "Jim's transfer papers are there."

"Transfer papers? I haven't seen anything about that," the director blustered.

"They're all in order," the specialist said mildly. "He'll be leaving with me this morning. In about two hours, less if I can make that happen."

The director didn't seem to know what to say.

The specialist said, "Go check your email. Make sure everything is in order, and, if you need any other signatures, I'll be here with my patient."

Lilianna watched the specialist with amusement—his overriding sense of power and might moving the director out to the hallway, closing the door behind him.

"You did that easily enough," she said. "I wish I could do that."

"It's understanding what your rights are and not letting somebody else walk all over them," the doctor said with a gentle smile. "We need to get the lawyers in here to get that POA matter settled. Then I want to take him away from here."

"As long as he's not gone for too long," she said swiftly. "We've got a hell of a mess, and everybody needs to know he's back, holding the reins in his hands."

"You can put the word out," the specialist said. "Particularly if investor confidence is an issue. Jim is definitely cognizant, but he'll need a little bit of time to get his head wrapped around his new reality. Imagine if you woke up to find your family fighting over your bones, and you're not dead yet, and everything's changed in the meantime, so you don't even have a home to go home to."

She nodded. "I know. Just so long as he's healthy. That's what I care about."

"Everybody needs to know they're loved," the specialist said.

Her father came out of the bathroom. "Okay, what's next?"

"I'll deal with the director, make sure all the paperwork is okay," Dr. Splicer said. "And Jonah will ship out the lab work immediately. I will call Gunner to let him know we'll be coming back to his place tonight."

Her father gave him a smile of relief. "And tell him that I'm really looking forward to seeing him."

The specialist stopped and looked at him. "Not as much as Gunner is looking forward to seeing you. You being gone for as long as you were has been hard on a lot of people."

Her father nodded. In a soft voice he said, "So I understand."

And with that the doctor and his nurse left.

Her father sat down on the side of the bed. "Any chance

of some food or at least a cup of coffee?"

Lilianna hopped to her feet. "My turn. I'll see what I can track down." She raced out of the room.

LIAM LOOKED OVER at Jim. "And, yes, there were tears in her eyes."

Jim nodded. "I just hadn't realized what a strain this must have been for her."

"That's what a couple days away from this place and your place will give you, a chance to get settled and grounded back in reality."

He sighed and said, "Keith was everything to me. I had three children, and I loved them all, but I never quite understood the girls. Keith was just like a mini-me. Losing him was so hard."

"Hard, yes, but your daughters lost not only a brother but they lost their father."

Jim winced. "I didn't do this on purpose."

"Of course not," Liam said quietly. "I'm not suggesting you did. But it's important to understand it wasn't just you who suffered. It's been a hardship on both your daughters too."

"Brianna is very much like her mother. She always looks out for number one."

"Well, now she has Carlos in the picture."

"And Carlos … I can't understand," Jim said. "I met him before Keith's death. He wasn't the kind of man I would have wanted for either of my daughters."

"Interesting that he was attracted to Lilianna first."

"Maybe. It just meant that Brianna wanted what Lilianna had. Brianna always did. She lacks self-confidence in a big way. Her way of handling it is to take from everybody else and to pretend to be bigger and better than the rest of the world. In many ways she's very good at what she does."

"What does she do?"

"She's in business," Jim said. "I presume she's the one who has taken over running the sanctuary."

"Some of it, yes. I don't know how effectively though. You need to understand just how little money has been coming in and how little money Lilianna has taken for her own needs. If the sanctuary can't handle paying for the expenses of those who work there, then you've got a problem."

"Most of us work for very little because we're working for the elephants. But you're right. You can't support too many paychecks. We have somebody who does a lot of the labor. I was a full-time employee. Keith was as well, but we had our own money so didn't take a paycheck. Lilianna was our biologist. We were looking to bring in more animals in need."

"Keith, did he have any friends or enemies?"

Jim smiled. "Sure, he may have had some enemies along the way, but he mostly had friends. Keith was a big teddy bear. He lived for the animals, just like I did."

"But you married and had three kids," Liam said. "What about Keith? Did he have a full-time girlfriend?"

Jim frowned as if trying to remember. "There was a girl, but I don't remember the details. I think he had just started dating her. I honestly don't remember. I hope there won't be big holes in my memory because that would be damn irritating."

"There probably will be for a while," Liam said. "It's hard to say. Don't get upset about it because there's only so much you can do right now. Don't expect so much these first few days."

"Right." Just then there was a knock on the door. Jim sighed. "It's bloody Grand Central Station in here."

The door opened before Liam had a chance to reach it. Inside stepped a man carrying a briefcase, wearing a three-piece suit.

Jim looked at him. "Eric?"

The man stopped. "Jim?"

Jim swung his legs off the bed and stood, walking over to greet Eric with his hand out. "Man, it's good to see you again."

Bewildered, Eric reached out and shook his hand. "I thought …" He stopped, confusion settling on his face.

"You thought what?" Liam asked, his tone hard. "You're the lawyer who tried to double-cross the family, aren't you?"

Eric shook his head. "I don't know what's going on," he said. "I was told you were comatose and that a power of attorney needed to be drawn up to keep the sanctuary solvent."

"Why are you here now?" Liam asked.

Eric shot him a resentful look. "Who the hell are you?"

"The name is Liam O'Brien," he said. "Not that you need my name because I have firsthand knowledge that Lilianna fired you as the lawyer for the sanctuary."

"She was just upset," Eric said. "I didn't take it serious-ly."

"Well, that's too damn bad, isn't it," Liam said, "because she already has another lawyer."

"What are you talking about?"

Jim stepped back slightly so he was more in between the two men. "Eric, you need to tell me what's going on."

Eric stared at him, almost dazed. "I can't believe you're actually"—he waved his hands—"you."

"Not only am I me," Jim said in a very forceful voice, "I'm back with full faculties, and I'm doing just fine, thank you. There'll be a full investigation as to why I was given drugs to keep me sedated and drugged out like a zombie."

Liam watched the confusion on the lawyer's face while figuring Jim out. Liam was almost willing to give the man the benefit of the doubt but not quite yet. "Brianna tried to establish power of attorney over her father. Is that or is that not correct?"

The lawyer nodded. "And that seems to be where the problem came in."

"Why would you do that?" Jim asked. "Why would you give her control of the estate?"

"Brianna said Lilianna didn't want to make those decisions. That she was too emotionally tied up and didn't want to have the power to make the decisions, whereas Brianna did want to," Eric explained. "And we all know Lilianna is very ..." His voice broke off.

"Very what?" Liam asked, his voice low but hard.

A flush crossed Eric's cheekbones. "She's delicate."

Liam's eyebrows shot up. "Like hell."

Eric stared at him. "What is your relationship with all this?"

"I'm the one who got this guy back on his feet. And I'm the one who will stop this chaos you appear to be in the middle of," Liam said in a hard voice. "I was brought in by Gunner, and no way in hell am I leaving until I get to the bottom of this."

Eric looked over at Jim. "You've spoken with Gunner?" There was hope in his voice.

Jim shook his head. "I will be talking to him today. I'm heading there this afternoon."

Eric's head just couldn't stop shaking from side to side, as if this was all too much for him. "You're leaving?"

Jim leaned forward. "Damn right I am. No way I'm staying here for somebody to continue drugging me. When I find out who's behind that, you can bet I'll be making sure they are behind bars."

There was such a look of horror on Eric's face that Liam had to wonder. "If your name is on any of those documents agreeing to have Jim drugged, you might as well start running now."

"I don't know what's going on," Eric said.

"All you need to know is that Lilianna's father was kept in a drugged state so other people could go for his asset base."

"But she swore he was incapable of even speaking clearly."

"Who swore that?"

"Lilianna," Eric said. "That's why, when she fired me, I figured she was just upset. We'd only spoken a few days earlier."

There was silence in the room as everybody tried to digest that.

Eric bit out, "See why I'm confused?"

"Not if you consider Brianna changes places with Lilianna at will," Liam said. "What do you want to bet it was Brianna who told you that?"

"But I spoke to the medical staff here too, and they said he wasn't cognizant of his surroundings. Or something like that." He shook his head. "It doesn't matter. And I don't know if it was Brianna or Lilianna now. I thought it was

Lilianna. But I'm not sure I asked."

"Of course not," Liam said smoothly. "And you should know better."

"I know I had one sister who asked for power of attorney. And one who wasn't interested."

"But did you confirm that with Lilianna?"

Eric looked at him. Fear was in the back of his eyes. "No. I'm not sure I did. I thought they were working together and never gave it a thought, figuring Brianna was just trying to help. No, but it never occurred to me that one sister would be trying to do something against the will of the other sister."

"It didn't occur to you?" Liam said in disgust. "This kind of shit happens all the time. Nobody ever wants to think the worst of somebody else."

"Of course not. Besides, the sisters can be very convincing."

"You mean Brianna can be very convincing," Jim said in a dry tone.

Eric turned his gaze to him. "I had to have seen both of them."

"Did you? Can you tell them apart?"

He frowned. "They have very different presences."

"Do you really think Brianna can't mimic Lilianna?"

"No. Brianna doesn't like to cower, and Lilianna doesn't have that kind of presence."

Liam watched as the door opened, but the lawyer didn't appear to hear the sound.

Lilianna frowned at the use of the word *cower*. She placed the tray down on the coffee table and slammed the door shut. The lawyer jumped. He turned, saw her and smiled. "There you are. Could you please explain to them what's going on here?"

"I'd love to," she said, "but I haven't a clue. How many times do you think you saw me over the last six months?"

He frowned.

"Who am I?"

"You're Lilianna."

"I am indeed," she said. "But I haven't seen you at all in six months."

Liam watched the lawyer's face intently. Liam saw the color blanch from Eric's complexion, and the man took a faltering half step backward.

Lilianna nodded. "And I will swear to that in a court of law."

He sat down on a nearby chair, completely shaken. Jim sighed, sat down on the couch and reached for a cup of coffee. "Wow. Sounds like your sister struck again."

"You have no idea what it's been like with you gone," Lilianna said. "The least you could have done was have two different-looking daughters."

"The least I could have done," her father said, "was had two daughters who took after me and none taking after your mother." The father and daughter looked at each other in sympathy.

Liam watched the whole circus. "How is it that you guys can be so calm about Brianna's behavior?" he asked. "At this point I'd be losing it."

"There's something very … determined about Brianna. She believes she's entitled to it all. She never wanted to be a twin."

"It doesn't matter if she wanted to be or not," Liam said. "I had a brother who thought he should have been an only child. He was physically abusive until I got big enough to fight back." His tone was hard. "And you can bet, once I could fight back, I did. The thing is, we don't always get what we want. But each of us deserves the right to live our lives in peace."

Lilianna nodded. "I guess I never learned to fight back."

Her father gently caught her fingers in his and held her hand close. "No, you have my personality. And I never could fight back with your mother either. And Brianna is your mother all over again."

"It wasn't much fun having her for a mom either," Lilianna said. "Keith and I were very close because of that."

Her father nodded. "Exactly why Keith and I bonded so well, and why you and I bonded, but it's hard to bond with Brianna. All I see is her mother."

"And yet she and Mother bonded. She came for the wedding. Do you know that Mom told me it was my fault that I lost my fiancé and how it served me right?" She waved a hand. "Obviously not in those words, but it was pretty damn close."

Her father sipped his coffee.

Liam just watched and waited for the lawyer to regain control of his voice. But the lawyer seemed to be almost in a comatose state. Good. It gave him a taste of his own medicine.

Chapter 9

LILIANNA LOOKED AT Eric. "You okay, Eric?"

"No," he said, his voice faint. "I'm not. I feel like I've been played."

"Sounds like you have been," her father said. "I warned you a long time ago how that girl was trouble."

Eric nodded. "You did. I just didn't see it coming."

"You never do," her father said. "I didn't see their mother come into my world either."

Everyone sat quietly.

Liam pulled up the spare chair and sat down.

Lilianna wasn't even sure what to say to him. This was so not what she'd brought him on board for. And they still hadn't gotten to the bottom of this. But, right now, her father's health was the priority.

The door opened yet again, and the specialist walked in. He looked at her father and said, "It's all set. You're being discharged." He glanced at his watch. "You need to be out of here by noon."

"Good," Jim said. "I want to get out of here. The sooner, the better."

The specialist looked over at Eric. "Who are you, and what relationship are you to my patient?"

Eric stared up at him. "I'm his friend, and I was his lawyer."

DALE MAYER

The specialist's eyebrows rose steeply. "Are you still his lawyer?"

Eric shook his head. "No, I don't think so. I'm afraid I haven't done well by him. Not by choice necessarily, but I have to consider the last six months and what may have gone on."

Another man walked into the room. Lilianna sighed. "I had no idea there was so much action in your bedroom, Father."

He chuckled. "Hopefully this will be over soon." Her father looked at the new arrival. "Harry, I haven't seen you in ages."

A big grin lit up Harry's face. "Now aren't you a sight for sore eyes? You're dressed. You're sitting. You're talking. Gunner will be more than pleased to see you like this."

Her father flushed. "Apparently the whole world thought I had disappeared."

Harry nodded, his gaze assessing and sharp. "Isn't that the truth?" He looked over at the other men. "Who is who?"

Liam straightened and shook his hand. "I'm Liam."

Harry nodded. "I'm Harry Stein, Gunner's attorney and now attorney of record for Jim, Lilianna and the sanctuary. Glad to see you've brought all this to a head." He looked over at the specialist. "Dr. Splicer, good to see you." The two men exchanged handshakes; then Harry turned to look at Eric, who even now was sitting with an aged expression on his face. "Eric? Tough day, huh?"

"I'll say," Eric said with feeling. "There have been some difficult revelations, but we have some things to discuss."

"One of the first is, where is Brianna?" Harry asked.

Lilianna gasped. "That's right. She was at the station." She turned to look at Eric. "Did you get her out of there?"

152

He gave her a sad smile and nodded. "Yes. I'm sorry. I didn't realize what was going on."

She sagged back on the couch. "Liam, you have to stay with my father. You have to make sure he's safe."

Liam shook his head. "No way Harry came alone. Not if there was any danger to Dr. Splicer, your father or even Harry himself. I highly suspect there'll be some men outside the door, waiting." He looked over at Harry. "Correct?"

Harry nodded and looked at Lilianna. "The local police are outside Jim's room. I also brought some enforcers of my own. No way Gunner wants to see you hurt either."

"She won't be," Liam said, his voice hard.

"And I'll be backing up Liam," North said, leaning negligently against the doorjamb.

Harry looked at him. "And who the hell are you?"

"I'm North. Liam and I have been here helping Lilianna."

"Good enough. Where do you want to do the paperwork? We have a lot to talk about."

"Better here so everybody is on board."

"The only one who doesn't need to be involved in these legalities is Dr. Splicer."

Dr. Splicer nodded. "I have some phone calls to make, so I'll give you twenty minutes, and then I'll come back. Good enough?"

Harry smiled. "If we can get this done in that short time, it would be the fastest legal lesson ever."

DR. SPLICER WALKED out at that moment.

Lilianna seemed to sag in place.

Liam walked around to stand between Eric and her with

North standing on the other side of the couch—bookends.

Harry nodded. "You'll stay and keep an eye on Lilianna?"

"We will. If you're taking her father to Gunner's place, he'll be safe. So we'll be with her."

"What the hell's going on?" she asked.

"According to the documentation and our conversation with Eric this morning," Harry said, "your sister has been trying to get power of attorney and sell a section of the sanctuary to a development company."

Jim cried out, "What?"

"Yes. She's had direct contact with a development company that wants the far section with the lake."

Her father shook his head. "There's no way. We need that water for the animals."

Lilianna looked at her father's new lawyer. "How far along in the process has she gotten?"

"I need to get a judge to hear the case, so we can put a stop to her shenanigans."

"Before Keith's accident," her father said slowly, "a company approached me about that land. I said absolutely no way. Keith was of the same mind. We needed the water rights and the land for the elephants. Plus, we were looking at bringing in more animals because we have the space."

Lilianna nodded. "I know that's the prettiest piece of all of the property."

"It's also closer to town. There's a main highway coming in soon that'll be not that far away from it, and they could put a huge development in there and make a lot of money," the lawyer said.

Eric seemed to sink deeper into the chair. "Dear God, what have I done?"

"Trying to sign away part of my property apparently," Jim roared. "What the hell, Eric?"

"I didn't know about this. I was trying to protect your estate, that's all," he cried out.

"Has anyone called the cops and picked up Brianna again?" Liam asked.

Harry pulled out his phone. "I'll get on that right now."

"Talk to Detective Olson," Liam said. "He's the one who took her away this morning. She should still be there, damn it." He glared at Eric, who seemed to cringe inside himself even more.

"Somebody needs to pick up her husband too," North said.

"Do you think Carlos is part of this?" Lilianna asked.

Jim looked at her. There was almost pity in his gaze. "Honey, Carlos was bad news right from the beginning."

She sighed. "I know. *Now.*"

"It didn't just start now," Jim said. "How long ago did they get married?"

She frowned. "Eighteen months ago. Mom came up to visit, about four or five months ago, and then I guess it wasn't long after that you apparently attacked the nurse and went straight downhill from there."

"Well, if somebody said I attacked your mother, and that's the reason I was drugged, I might believe them," he said with a dry tone. "That woman can set me off faster than anybody." He frowned. "Actually …" He shook his head. "Can somebody check if she came to see me? Because I have in my head a huge fight. I can't tell what's real and what's not real."

North said, "I'm on it." He slipped out of the room.

Jim stared at the door. "He's quiet."

"He's also very good," Liam said. "But we need to ensure none of your sanctuary land changes hands, stopping the sale from being registered. Because not only will the land be gone but you know the money'll be gone too."

The lawyer was over at the window, having a hard and fast conversation. When he hung up, he turned. "The cops are looking for Brianna now." His voice droned on as he made several calls, getting other people in on the action.

Jim sat there, his hands in front of him. "She wouldn't just take the land away from me, would she?"

"You might want to consider the fact that, as far as she's concerned, it wouldn't be taking it from you at all," Lilianna said. "She never thought the elephants needed as much space as they have, and that was always the space brought up in the past for sale. If she thought that land was of interest to developers, then it would make sense she might be after it now."

"Carlos and she both came to my office," Eric said. "That's why I knew it was Brianna. Because she was there with her husband."

"Then he wasn't there sometimes?"

He turned a dazed look toward her. "Right. And she had clothes more like you wear. They were quieter, softer. Her hair would be in a braid, like you always wear. When she was with him, it was always curls and waves and makeup. She appeared completely different."

Liam almost felt sorry for Eric. Brianna had pulled a fast one on him, and, instead of being someone who was defending Jim's land and looking after the daughters' future, he'd been duped.

Eric shook his head as he seemed to be putting the puzzle pieces together. "They were working on a tight time frame. The medications had to be administered long enough to prove your father wasn't improving. Then a POA application could be rushed through, and the property deal signed as soon as possible. They had to complete these steps before Lilianna found out about the POA and launched a legal challenge to stop the property sale. Oh, my God …"

Liam watched as Jim turned tortured eyes to Lilianna.

She grabbed her father's hands. "Steady. We've spent a lot of time getting you to this point. We have help now. We've caught this in time. Let us sort it out. You just stay strong."

Liam wished it would be that simple. But he had given up believing in fairy tales a long time ago.

Chapter 10

LILIANNA COULDN'T BELIEVE how fast things were moving now. The lawyers were into heavy discussions. The specialist was getting everything tidied up so her father could go to Gunner's place. She looked to Liam. "Do we go to Gunner's too?"

He shook his head. "What I really want to do is search your sister's house. But I need permission."

Jim looked up and said, "It's my house. You have my permission."

Liam turned to both lawyers, then back to Lilianna. "Would you feel better if you followed your father to Gunner's home?" He leaned over and grabbed her hand. "And that's okay if that's how you feel. But, at the same time, I do need to go through the main house."

The lawyers at that moment split apart. "We'll draw up a document right now, giving you the right to enter the premises. The property still belongs to Jim."

"Damn right it does," Jim said, his voice strident, angry. "And they sure as hell better not have done anything to have changed that."

"We're working on it," Harry said. He brought out a pad of paper and drafted a simple document. He handed it to Jim. "Sign this."

Jim read it, signed it and handed to Lilianna. She looked

at it, saw she was required to sign it and did so. Then Harry and Eric signed as witnesses.

"So that covers everybody except Brianna," Liam joked. But it fell flat in the air.

Lilianna shook her head. "She won't like this."

"Doesn't matter if she does or not," Harry said. "We need to investigate the last two years of the sanctuary's business dealings to see if she's done anything else, like steal funds."

"The accountant should be able to tell us that," Lilianna said.

At that her father raised his head. "Please tell me Joseph is still handling the accounts."

She shook her head. "No, Joseph retired, Dad. We have McCormick and Sons handling it."

Her father stared at her. "Oh no. Joseph has to handle it. I can't trust anybody else."

"Dad, when you went under, Joseph struggled to do anything. He was so upset. He was already over sixty, and he didn't want to do it anymore."

"Call him," Jim said. "We'll get him to take a look at the books to make sure there's been no shenanigans since he handed them off."

Lilianna pulled out her phone. "Here. I've dialed Joseph's number. You talk to him. It's on Speaker." She handed her father the phone.

He took it hesitantly, but, when Joseph's voice rang through, he smiled. "Joseph, this is Jim."

There was a shocked silence on the other end, and then Joseph said, "Oh, my God! Is that really you?"

She listened as the man did a quick welcome back.

Then her father said clearly, "I need you to take a look at

the sanctuary's books. I'm afraid something may have gone wrong since you stepped down."

"I'm retired. You know that, right?"

Her father nodded. "So Lilianna says. But I'm afraid my daughter's done something wrong."

Joseph groaned. "And that would be Brianna. If there was ever one who would cause you trouble, it was that one."

"I know, and you warned me about it. But I've been out of circulation for a couple years now."

"Yeah, and that was the damnedest thing," Joseph said. "I have to admit, my heart wasn't in handling the books after that."

"I really need you to give me a hand getting back to life. I'm only now feeling better, and I find out I've been drugged for four months, at least, if not for two years, and now I'm trying to regain control before my daughter steals everything."

"Can you send me the log-ins?"

Her father turned toward Lilianna, and she shrugged. "I can try to find them, but Brianna's probably changed them. I have some paper copies, or at least they're at the office."

Liam stood. "We'll go to the office now," he said quietly. "And then we'll search the house so we can get at least that much information. And I don't give a damn who is there."

Lilianna looked up at him. "I'm coming too. I want to check on the dogs, and I'll check the bank records while I'm there."

Her father, his voice low, said, "Email them to Joseph, please."

Joseph thanked everyone.

"I can do that." At that she stood. "I need my phone back. We've made our plans with Joseph. We'll get you a phone too, Dad. But, in the meantime"—she extended her hand, palm up, and her father handed over her phone—"Joseph can use my phone as a contact for you. Until we get a full picture, I don't know how bad things are."

"I'll stand by," Joseph said, his voice invigorated. "Damn, Lilianna, your father is back!"

She chuckled. "And honestly that's the best gift ever."

She bent down, kissed her father on the cheek, turned to glare at Harry. "You promise he'll be safe?"

Harry nodded. He turned to Liam. "Send in my men, will you? They are out in the parking lot, waiting for me."

Liam nodded. "Will do." He waited for Lilianna to join him at the doorway, where, outside stood four uniformed officers. Liam acknowledged them with a silent raise of his chin, and Liam and Lilianna walked to the front entrance. Katie was still at the reception desk.

Lilianna walked over to her. "Don't you get to go home today?"

Katie groaned. "Maria quit. I finally reached her by phone, and she said she was sick. Then I said Lilianna wanted to talk to Maria, about Mr. Howell." Katie sighed. "Maria seemed okay with it. Then she called back and handed in her notice."

Liam stepped forward. "The police will want to speak to her about the attack on her."

Katie bit her bottom lip. "Police? Isn't that a bit extreme?"

"No, not at this point. It needs to be addressed."

Lilianna added in a low tone, "I don't know what's going on here, Katie, but it's bad news. So please, don't say anything to anyone."

Outside Liam walked to the large black car and tapped

on the heavily tinted window. The window rolled down. "Mr. Stein wants you inside," he said.

The driver nodded and turned to look at the passenger. Both hopped out, and the closest one asked, "What room is he in?"

"Room 104," Lilianna said. "He's with my father. Please take good care of him."

Both men nodded. "Will do."

She turned to look at Liam. "Where is North, and where is the truck?"

Just then North came out the front door. "Jeez, you two are always on the move," he said with a smile.

Liam gave him a droll look. "Yeah, we moved from the room to the front entrance. That's it for how many hours now?"

North motioned toward the truck. "Where we going?"

"The office first," Lilianna said. "I need to get whatever accounting stuff I can find and collect the dogs too."

Liam added, "We have a signed letter giving me permission to go into the main house and the office and search them. Not to mention pull financial information."

"Wow." North whistled. "That'll be fun. And by the way, there is a record of your mother coming in to visit your father, just before he supposedly attacked a nurse."

Lilianna gasped. "That would make more sense than anything. She always set him off. Use Maria to file a complaint and it's a done deal. When the doctors see my father, he'd still be agitated."

"A perfect situation to take advantage of and further their agenda," North added.

"Makes sense," Liam said. "Still shitty though."

"I don't know what the deal is with this Carlos," North

said. "As far as I can see, he's a ghost."

Lilianna turned to look at him in surprise. "Isn't that who you saw last night at my cabin?"

"I don't know who I saw last night." He turned to look at Liam. "Gunner's man brought a bug detector for us too."

"Oh, good. While I'm checking out the office, you can test the office and then maybe do a run-through of the cabin."

"Will do."

"I thought you had something with you," she said.

"No. We didn't bring it with us," Liam said. "We also don't have any place to put all our stuff, including yours, Lilianna, which is now in the truck."

She looked in the back to see the bed was full and sighed as she pulled the cover closed. "My entire life has boiled down to this."

The men nodded but didn't try to make light of it. After all, what could anybody say? Her life had come to this, not easily and not fast, but it was a mess.

They made it back to the sanctuary property in no time. Lilianna was surprised to see the speed with which they got her home. But instead of going around to her cabin where the dogs were, Liam hopped out at the office.

"Who else is here?" he asked.

"There's the usual staff looking after the elephants," she said. "The question is whether my sister is here or not."

"Let's go find out," he said.

They walked into the tourist building and found Daniel stacking brochures for visitors. He looked up and smiled. "Wow. It's been hard to round anybody up today."

"Sorry, I've been off the premises all day."

Daniel chuckled. "That's okay. I'm used to it. It's a good

thing we didn't have any tours or anything."

"How are the elephants?"

"They're fine. I'm just running out for some fresh food. We got a delivery from one of the markets, a couple wagons full of watermelons and squashes."

She clapped her hands with delight. "Oh, my goodness! They'll love that." She turned to look at Liam. "They adore melons."

Daniel said, "I can wait half an hour or so if you want to come out with me."

She sighed. "I've got so much going on right now, so that's not happening. Can you hold back some of the melons for tomorrow or the next day?"

He nodded. "They're not all that overripe yet. I'll take some today. I don't know, maybe sixty or seventy, and see how they do."

"Sixty or seventy?" Liam asked.

Daniel laughed. "You haven't seen these elephants eat." He headed out the back door.

Liam asked in a low voice, "You don't want to ask where your sister is?"

She frowned and raced to the door. "Daniel, do you know where my sister is?"

He shook his head. "I saw her head off about an hour ago. I haven't seen her come back yet."

She gave him a wave goodbye.

Liam nodded and said, "In that case, I'm heading to the house. Let's take a quick look at the office first."

She went into the office and pulled out ledgers. "These arc all blank."

"Keep looking," he said urgently.

She searched the office files. "There's nothing here."

"Check online."

She logged on to the computer. "I'm still locked out of the accounting program. Brianna said she would reset the password." She frowned. "I gather it was foolish of me to believe her." She called Daniel. "I can't get into the accounting program. Can I use your log-in?"

"Sure." He recited it for her, and she punched in the information.

"Okay, it's letting me in. Thanks."

"No problem. Double-check your access. You probably just need to change your password, and it should be fine."

Lilianna disconnected the call. She'd check that later. Right now, she was in, and *there* was the information she sought.

"Print that off," Liam said over her shoulder. "You want both a hard copy and a digital copy."

Following his instructions, she printed several pages from the last six months and then created a PDF of the whole thing and downloaded it in her Excel program so she had something she could import into another program. "Okay, got all that."

"Email it to Joseph."

That took a little bit longer, but finally she said, "Okay."

"Now get into the sanctuary's bank account and download as many statements as you can covering the last two years. Three years would be better, so we could see what the normal revenue should be as compared to now. We need to get an idea of what's going on."

"I've been in here lots," she said bewildered. "I just never thought to look for anything untoward."

"Exactly why there's a problem," he said. "When you're not expecting anything to go wrong, you aren't looking for problems. But once they happen …"

She nodded. "I'm almost done here, but I'd like to spend a few minutes and go through some of the emails." She looked up at him. "Are you okay to go through the house on your own, or do you want me to come?"

"Better that you don't come," he said with a smile. "In case you hadn't noticed, North has already scanned the office, and he's gone up to scan your cabin now. But, if you see your sister, call me. If you hear anything, send me a warning." Just then his phone went off. He pulled it out and raised an eyebrow. "It's Detective Olson." He walked a few steps away. "Liam here."

The conversation was short but intense before he turned back to her, his face was grim. "He spoke to Maria who confessed to taking a payout to lodge a fabricated complaint against your father."

Outrage whipped through her. "That's just so wrong."

"She didn't want to say who paid her, but, with some pressure, she admitted it was Carlos." He gave her a quick hug. "Don't dwell on it. We'll get this all sorted."

There was nothing anybody could say that could take away the pain of such a betrayal hitting her. She nodded in acknowledgment. Biting her lower lip, she walked with Liam to the back door and watched as he headed to the main house.

She held no ill will toward her sister, although a part of her wondered why she didn't. Her sister needed to get the hell off the land and go find a life of her own though. Then again, maybe Lilianna should take her own advice.

Just then her phone rang. She glanced down, seeing it was her mother. Frowning, she answered, "Mom, what's up?"

"You mean, I can't just call and say hi?" her mother asked in a testy voice.

Lilianna pinched the bridge of her nose. If there was one thing about her mother, the answer to that question was no. This woman always wanted *something*.

"So why did you call?"

"Brianna has been telling me all kinds of horror stories. She was in tears, I tell you, tears," her mother cried out. "Do you realize she was almost arrested?"

"No, I didn't realize that," Lilianna said smoothly. "Hopefully she got it all sorted out. I've been with Dad all day."

"Why do you want to sit beside that old empty bag?" her mother snorted. "He didn't have a whole lot in the years when I was married to him, which made it easier to get out when I wanted, but now he's completely useless. Honestly he should have just committed suicide instead of costing so much money by sticking around."

Lilianna pinched her lips together. "I happen to love my father very much," she said, gritting her teeth with unnecessary force. "Did you have a reason for calling?"

"*Pfff*, course I had a reason for calling," her mother yelled. "I want to know what you're up to. Brianna says you've gone completely against her."

"I haven't said two words to Brianna in the last twenty-four hours. What are you talking about?" Inside she wished she could get her mother to say anything that would give her an idea what was going on.

"Well, that's not what Brianna says."

"And of course, if Brianna says something, Brianna is telling the truth, and I'm not." Lilianna sighed. "Same old story, Mom. So why are you calling me if you're not pumping me for information?"

There was a long silence on the other end. "Is that what you think of me?" her mother said with a false hurt tone.

"Mom, get to the point."

"The point is, somebody is trying to hurt Brianna, and I want to make sure it's not you."

"Why would I do anything to hurt my sister?"

"I don't know. That's why I'm asking."

"Did you ask Brianna if she's done anything to hurt me?" Lilianna asked.

"No, of course not. Your sister would never hurt you. Nor would she hurt anybody."

"Really? That's why she slept with my fiancé, right?" Lilianna winced. She should never have mentioned that to her mother. It just gave her mother an opening to pounce on.

And sure enough her mother cried out, "You're not still holding that against her, are you? You can't stop true love, honey. I'm so sorry you're feeling heartbroken and lost without him. But he obviously wasn't yours to begin with if she could take him away from you so easily."

"Whatever, Mom."

"Is this what this is all about? Is it that you've finally got an opportunity to pay your sister back?" her mother cried out, her voice rising in a crescendo.

Lilianna rolled her eyes. She rose and paced the office, going down the hallway and out to the tourist area where they had all the brochures on the elephants and on how to set up for the tours. "No, Mom, this has nothing to do with Brianna."

"What does it have to do with?" Her mother sniffed. "I can't believe you'd do something to hurt your sister."

"I haven't done anything to hurt my sister. You're not listening to me," Lilianna said, her voice hardening at the end. "You never listen to me. Maybe you should be telling me what Brianna is up to. But then again, maybe you're up to the same damn thing?"

"Don't you swear at me," her mom said in an ominous tone.

Lilianna laughed. "I hardly think saying the word *damn* is the issue at the moment."

"That's not how you talk to your mother."

"It is if my mother is only trying to cause trouble," Lilianna said. "So what the hell is my sister up to?"

"What makes you think she's up to anything?" her mother said, then, as if trying to change tactics, asked, "What are you thinking she's up to?"

Lilianna leaned against the front door and smiled. "There you go, fishing for information again."

"Obviously you're in a mood," her mom said with a sniff. "I'll call back later." And she hung up.

Lilianna stared at the phone. She wanted to say, *good riddance.* The trouble was, the woman was still her mother. And it was damn hard to let go of any of the memories. All the memories were still tied up with her father, and that just reminded her how much her father had already been through. Had her mother had anything to do with all this? And, if so, why?

The answers wouldn't be found on the front doorstep, but she did have access to her sister's email. If her password was still the same. Brianna hated changing her passwords.

Lilianna returned to the computer and logged in. Perfect. It was still her last name and birthdate. Checking her sister's email was an invasion of privacy, but, given the circumstances, Lilianna wouldn't feel guilty about it. Once there, she checked for emails from her mother.

And sure enough, there were dozens of them. Lilianna glanced through several and frowned as she realized what was going on. They were trying to sell part of the property to the development company. Her mother had suggested it, apparently sometime around the wedding.

Lilianna didn't quite know what to do with the emails. She saved them onto a USB drive and checked for emails between her sister and the development company. By the time she was done, she was furiously angry. But she had a ton of material on a key, and she had forwarded a ton of the emails to the lawyers. Hopefully somebody could stop her sister and fast.

She heard a door open and close out front. She logged into her own account and, with the stack of paperwork in a folder in front of her, she waited to see who would come in.

Her sister flounced into the office, only to stop and stare at Lilianna sitting at the desk. "What are you doing here?"

Lilianna looked up. "What are you talking about? Why shouldn't I be here?"

Her sister dropped her purse. "I don't know what the hell is going on, but my life is terrible," she wailed. "That police officer took me down to the station and interrogated me."

"Interesting," Lilianna said smoothly. "What did you do?"

"I didn't do anything," her sister roared. "Didn't you hear me?"

"No, I was too busy spending time with Dad," Lilianna said with a smile.

"That old geezer. He should just kick the bucket before

we lose every penny we have to that old-folks' home."

Lilianna stared at her. "And maybe you and Mom did something a few months ago to speed that up, huh?"

Her sister took a stumbling step forward and then collapsed in the chair. "What are you talking about?"

"Oh, I think you know," Lilianna said with a hard smile.

LIAM STEPPED INSIDE the empty house and took a moment to listen. There were no sounds of the living. No creaks, no voices, nothing to say anybody was home. But he'd been fooled before. The last thing he wanted was to appear like an intruder. He called out, "Hello?"

No answer. He walked through the lower part of the house, quickly assessing what was on each floor. The ground floor was a standard layout with a dining room, living room, kitchen, bathroom, and in the back corner was an office. It had French doors leading out onto a deck. Upstairs he found the master bedroom, obviously occupied by the couple living here, and three spare bedrooms, all empty. He took a moment to check the closets, but they held nothing but linens. In that case, what had happened to Jim's clothing and personal belongings?

Frowning, and not liking where his thoughts were taking him, he returned downstairs, headed for the office. If there was any information to be had, it would likely come from there. He sat down at the desk and booted up the laptop and desktop computers. Both were still on, had just been in Sleep mode. He hit Enter and got into the desktop.

The laptop required a password. He left that one for the moment and clicked through the desktop to see what he could find. He was aware of the passage of time. He didn't know how long he'd have alone. And there were not only the computers to deal with but he wanted to check the nearby file cabinet. He checked the folders in the main hard drive, saw no USBs or anything else attached and put a USB key in himself. The hard drive had a lot of different folders with business type names.

He copied everything onto the USB and then tried to bring up email. That was locked. Of course it was. He checked the icons on the desktop, but only a couple were folders sitting in plain sight. He copied those as well and then turned his attention to the desk's drawers. In the top middle drawer were pencils, pens, the usual junk everybody tossed in. On the left side, the second drawer was enough to make him give a soundless whistle. Stacks of cash and a handgun.

He pulled out his phone and took a photo and then lifted the gun, checked to see if any bullets were in the barrel and emptied it. He wiped it clean of his fingerprints, replaced it, took a solid look at the money and realized there had to be at least twenty thousand cash in this one drawer. Interesting to have so much money lying around the house when the sanctuary was struggling. But then Carlos was a businessman, and there was no reason for his business to integrate with the sanctuary, other than a husband helping out his wife during a downturn. On the right side of the desk, Liam pulled out the top drawer and found stacks of folders lying inside that were obviously current projects.

The first contained only a couple pages. He didn't have the time to look at them; he just took photos of the contents of each folder, so that he could enlarge them later, once he got them uploaded into the special program on his laptop. The next drawer down was a file drawer with four or five hanging folders.

Feeling the edge of time bite at him, he took as many photos as he could, closed the file drawer and moved to the filing cabinet against the wall, only to find it was locked. Swearing softly, he checked the walls and found a safe behind one of the paintings. It was obviously not a new addition to the house, so something Jim should be able to access—unless Brianna and Carlos had changed the combination. Liam sent the lawyer a text, asking Jim for the combination.

In the meantime, Liam did a full sweep of the rest of the office, quickly planting two bugs. He could only hope they would go unnoticed. What he wanted to do was get back upstairs to the master bedroom and place a bug in there too.

As soon as he was done here, he ran upstairs, planted the bug behind the headboard and came back down. Outside, he saw somebody walking toward the house.

A quick glance confirmed it was Brianna. Her strides were just as long and mile-eating as Lilianna's, but there was a clip of anger to hers. Liam stepped out the rear exit of the home office, through the French doors to a backyard deck, and ran for the trees up along the right side of the house. He heard the door of the house close as she slammed it behind her and realized just how close he'd come to getting caught. Keeping to the trees, he went over the rise and headed for the cabin. The dogs greeted him joyfully. He walked inside to find North online already. "How many bugs did you find here?"

"Three. And you have three up and running at the house," North said quietly.

"I wanted to get one in the kitchen, but I didn't have any left."

"We might get another opportunity."

"What we really need," Liam said, "is something to break in this case. How about they come home and have a fight, giving us the juicy details of their plan?" With a shake of his head, he shared what he'd found in the house. "There's no sign of her father's belongings. No clothing, nothing. It's like they completely took over his house and thought he'd never come back."

"If we're fair, her father did appear to be declining at a very rapid rate. It's not all that hard to imagine they thought the house was theirs."

"Hardly fair, if Lilianna is in a small cabin like this, and they get a big house."

North shrugged. "Doesn't sound like Brianna has been fair about anything. It's more a case of *take what they want and to hell with anybody else.*"

Liam nodded. "I presume you've left the bugs in place here but shut them down?"

North nodded. "Yes." Just then a voice came through his laptop.

North and Liam sat back and listened as Brianna's voice filled the cabin.

"Look. I don't know what's going on, but obviously they have some idea something's up," she snapped.

They couldn't hear a response or anybody else talking, so Liam assumed she was on the phone.

"No. No. Lilianna didn't ask me anything like that, but she was different. More confident. I don't know what's going on. And I don't know why the hell she thought she could bring in those two goons." And then her voice relaxed. "I know. I know. I'm just irate. I spent all morning at the police station. They were asking me all kinds of questions.

There will obviously be some kind of an investigation into the sanctuary." She groaned, a hard, irritated sound. "No, I didn't say anything about our business. No, I didn't say anything about the development project. I just told the detective to contact my lawyer. And, yes, Eric did show up finally," she snapped. "I swear to God, I was there for at least an hour before he arrived."

There was silence, and they could imagine her listening. She snorted every once in a while, and then she gasped. The two men both wished they could hear the other half of her conversation.

"You said the paperwork was all in order. I signed everything, so what else is there we possibly need to do? It doesn't matter if they try to stop us. Everything's completed, right?" When there was silence for a moment longer, she said, her voice rising, "Right? ... What do you mean, you don't know? That you left it with the lawyers to finish?"

There was a sound of clipped footsteps as if she were pacing through the house. But her voice didn't drain away, so she was pacing the office.

"Look. You need to find out what the hell is going on. It's one thing for them to come back at us afterward and say, *Hey, what did you do? We'll prove you did something wrong,* but it's another thing entirely for them to stop the process beforehand because we'll never get ownership of this place if that happens. And, if that happens, we won't complete the deal with the damn development company either."

Just then Liam heard a nearby gasp, and he looked up to see Lilianna standing in the doorway of her cabin, the dogs weaving around her legs. She'd heard her sister's voice through the laptop. She stared at him, her eyes huge.

He lifted a finger to his lips, and she nodded, placed her

bag with her own laptop and purse on the kitchen counter and came to stand behind North.

"No. I know. I know. I won't say anything to anybody. Look. Either you come home, or I need to come into town. You decide." Then she changed her mind. "No. I'll just come in. This place feels creepy enough now. I can't wait until we can sell the whole goddamn thing. I'll be there in about forty-five minutes. I'll pack a bag and stay overnight. Do you want me to bring you anything?"

And there followed a laundry list she repeated back of what was required for the overnight stay.

"Book us a hotel room, will you? Unless you want to stay at the penthouse suite. But you said it was being renovated still." Silence again. "Fine then, book us the hotel room," she snapped.

And she hung up, or at least they assumed she'd hung up. There was silence for a moment, followed by sounds of papers rustling, clicking on the keyboard, and then she exclaimed, "What the hell? I need to get going. I'm so late already."

They heard a chair being pushed back and Brianna bolting from the room. In a minute, there were sounds coming from the other bug in the master suite as she packed up clothing, muttering to herself.

"I don't have time to pack his shit. This should have been put to rest already. He damn well better be doing his job. And why aren't the renovations done? We're supposed to have moved already."

It was all very interesting, though had nothing to do with the problems at the sanctuary, but had an awful lot to do with understanding her mind-set. They listened until she was done, approximately fifteen minutes, and then there were sounds of bags being carried.

After she slammed the front door shut, no more was heard.

Lilianna raced upstairs to the loft. Liam followed her. She looked out the window to see her sister driving slowly down the driveway toward the highway. She turned to look at Liam. "You put bugs in the main house?"

"I did. Two in the office. One in the master bedroom. I wanted to get a fourth one in the kitchen, but I didn't have another."

"She always acts like she has nothing to do with anything. Then you hear this ... What penthouse? When I knew Carlos, he didn't have anything like that."

"You said he was an investment advisor. They're usually very well paid."

Confused, she said, "I know, but, at that time, he told me that he didn't own any property. Maybe he just didn't want to let me know what he had because he was afraid I would take advantage ..."

"Or he's taking the money coming into the sanctuary and using that to complete his penthouse. Obviously Brianna would much prefer a penthouse to staying here in an old house and looking after the elephants."

She nodded. "How sad is that?"

"You also should know the results of my house search," he said. "Obviously I didn't have time for a full search, but I couldn't find any sign of your father's clothing or personal belongings."

She turned to face Liam, her mind working, her lips thinning. "Then they'll be in the basement most likely. But there's no guarantee she even kept them."

"She's gone now. Shall we take a look?"

She hesitated as if still warring with the idea she shouldn't be allowed in the main house, and then she nodded. "Yes, we need to. I have to find out what my dad wants to do too. He's supposed to be staying at Gunner's. But I can easily see him deciding, if Brianna and Carlos aren't coming back tonight, then maybe he should move back home again."

"Maybe that wouldn't be a bad thing, especially if Gunner can lend a couple men to bring him home."

"And stay here for a few days," she said drily.

"Until everything is fine again, yes."

She nodded and glanced at North. "Do you want to come too?"

"Absolutely," North said with a big grin. He jumped to his feet. "Nothing I like better than snooping around other people's houses."

She shot him a look, but Liam laughed and gently stroked her shoulder. "Easy. We're only joking."

She nodded. "I'm sorry. I'm just so touchy. It seems I haven't slept in weeks."

"Let's take a look at the house again and see what we can find." He walked toward the front door, holding her close. "Does your sister keep much money in the house?"

"I don't think so. We never had much money."

"Did Carlos ever live with you?"

"No, but he spent the night often."

"Did you ever see him with large amounts of cash?"

She shook her head. "No."

"Do you know how to get into the safe?"

She gave him a startled look. "You found the safe?"

"Of course," he said. "I also found a large amount of cash and a handgun in the desk in the home office."

She stopped. "What?"

He shrugged. "I was going to ask you about it."

She stared at him. "As far as I know, my father has two rifles. I don't know anything about a handgun. This is Texas. Most of us are armed," she said, her tone short. "But I don't think he ever kept anything in the office, and none of us ever had cash."

"Let's take a look," Liam said, "and we'll see if you recognize the gun."

He held out his hand.

Chapter 11

LILIANNA DIDN'T KNOW why, yet it was instinctive to grasp Liam's hand. It was like a lifeline. Somebody understood what she was going through. Somebody way too attractive for her peace of mind. He'd been a godsend these last couple days. She'd had no idea what she'd set in motion when she had contacted Gunner a few days back. She couldn't imagine the depth of the ugliness she'd found.

And yet a constant throughout the last two days was Liam. Honest, with integrity, standing stalwart in the face of all kinds of evil. She hated to think he'd spent his life with so much of this same kind of nastiness. "You couldn't have had an easy life if all of this is commonplace for you." She studied his face as he glanced at her.

A smile kinked up the corners of his lips. "The thing about life is, you get to decide how you want to deal with it. You can stand still and let things run all over you, or you can step up and do your part to stop it. After years in the military of doing my part to step up, it's a whole lot easier to recognize when somebody else is trying to be an absolute shit."

She nodded. "And I guess that's one of the things I struggle with, isn't it? I had no idea anybody would do something like this."

"There's always somebody out there ready to take advantage. While your father was at the helm, they saw him as a strong, capable, honest person, doing his best to help the elephants. In your case, there was no one designated person at the helm anymore. It was either your sister or you, but one of you needs to be the dominant figurehead. The sanctuary needed that."

"You think Carlos is behind this?"

"I want it to be so to take your sister out of equation," he said, "but it sounds to me like she's just as deep in this as he is. In the past has she spent much time with the elephants?"

"All of us did. But it was my father's thing. My sister had already left home before he got heavily into it."

"Where did she go?"

"She moved in with my mom for a few years. Got married and then got divorced," she said with a wince. "That marriage lasted about six months." She walked another few paces and said, "I hope she didn't plan it that way."

"I don't know. What do you think about your sister?"

"She's one of those people who gets what she wants. But I'm not sure she cares about who she steps on to get it," Lilianna said. "And that's a terrible thing to say about a sibling. Especially a twin."

She stumbled on a rock. Instantly his arm reached out and caught her. She stood for a moment, steadied herself as the dogs milled around them both. North stepped around them and continued walking ahead. She wasn't sure if he was trying to give them time alone. When he was a good ten yards ahead of her, she stepped on her foot again and kind of winced. "It'll be fine," she said. "I guess I rolled my ankle slightly."

"Are you okay to keep walking?"

She took a few tentative steps and then nodded. "Yes. I'll

be fine." She tried to use determination and confidence. But it was hard. Her muscles cringed every time she took a step. She shook out her ankle again and took several more steps. "I just need to be careful."

He held out his arm, wrapped it around her so she was hanging on for support. "Take the support when you have it," he said gently. "You won't hurt me by leaning on me."

She could believe that. The man was built like a bloody tree trunk.

They walked slowly down the hill toward the main house. By the time they were halfway there, North was already stepping in the back patio doors.

"Normally those are locked," she said frowning.

"You can put that down to me," Liam said. "I came out that way when your sister came in."

She nodded. "Brianna wouldn't have noticed. She's not very good at noticing details."

"What does she do well then?"

"She's very good at schmoozing," Lilianna confessed.

"What good will that do if you're the one who's out there trying to drum up money?"

"I didn't want that position," Lilianna said. "That was my father's gift, and Brianna was very good at it too. But Brianna said she didn't want to do it anymore. She wanted to stay and handle all the books."

"And so you let her?"

"It seems like I've let a lot of people do a lot of things in my life that I'm not really happy about now. Or then," she said.

He chuckled. "Doesn't sound like you're being very shy and retiring with me."

"I've always been weak." And she hated it.

His voice was gentle but firm. "I don't think you're weak. I don't think you're a victim. I do think that life got ahead of you, and you didn't understand what was happening until too late."

She gave a quick nod. "But I'm not naive," she muttered. "I just want to believe the best of people." She could see he was almost biting his lips to hold back his comment, and she laughed. "Okay, so that means I'm naive." She shrugged. "I'm not alone in the world."

"Absolutely you're not," he said with a gentle smile. "And we need people like you. The world needs more gentle givers. There are enough harsh takers out there. The givers need to be protected. They need to be honored. Too often they're lost in the shuffle as everybody does a power grab around them, ignoring that they have value, that they need to be appreciated for who they are."

His words struck home in a big way. She'd never heard it told in such a manner. And it certainly wasn't what she expected from somebody like him. But then she had to question her own stereotypical attitude. What did she mean by a somebody like him? "I've never thought about it that way," she said quietly. They were almost at the house. She looked around at it. "This was my home. But once Carlos had an affair with my sister, I couldn't get out fast enough."

"And it will always have that taint to it for you. But you can't let it ruin your life."

"Of course I haven't let it ruin my life," she cried out.

"Have you had a relationship since?"

Inside, she shriveled a little. She shook her head. "No, but not because I was afraid of men. More because I was afraid I'd make another bad choice. I thought I could trust him. I thought he wanted to be with me."

"And, at the time, he probably did," Liam said. "Did you consider he was attracted to you, but Brianna just knocked him sideways?"

"You mean, love at first sight or something stupid like that?" And then she corrected herself. "No, love at first sight is not stupid. Of course it isn't. But I wonder if he never loved me. Once he had a chance to meet Brianna and see how much more dynamic she was, then he was attracted to her."

"And it's possible he didn't know his own mind. I want to give the guy the benefit of the doubt," Liam said. "It's got to be a little daunting to realize you're with one sister, but you really want the other one."

"Particularly daunting for the sister involved at the time too," she said with a sigh. "And I haven't tried to avoid relationships. But I haven't gone looking for one either."

"Right. Because, when you lack confidence in your own judgment, it's hard to trust again, isn't it?"

"I don't think it's hard to trust men. I think it's hard to trust myself."

"That's normal," he said. "But, as soon as you think you're ready to trust that little voice again, let me know."

Startled, she stared at him. "Why is that?" She drew her eyebrows together.

He gave her a lopsided look. "Because I'd like to show you that not all men are like Carlos."

She stopped in her tracks. "Are you suggesting you would like to go out with me?"

He chuckled. "I'd like to do a whole lot more than that," he said with bald honesty. "But you're a long way away from being ready for such a relationship."

But she wasn't. In the back of her head she knew she

wasn't. Her only stumbling block had been she hadn't found another man she thought she could trust, who was worthy of her trust. She fisted her hands on her hips and glared at him. "How do you know I'm a long way away from that?"

He studied her for a moment. "Because you still seem to be pining for Carlos."

And then she gave a defiant shake of her head. "I'm *so* not longing for Carlos. That was over the moment I found him in bed with my sister. For me, trust is a huge part of a relationship. If there's no honesty, there's no trust. And, if there's no trust, there can't be any love."

He nodded. "Glad to hear that." She glared at him for a long moment, until he raised his eyebrows and asked, "So now what are you mad at?"

"Well, now you're supposed to ask me out," she said in frustration, not sure what she was doing.

He chuckled. "While you're spouting all kinds of stuff, why don't you invite me out?" he challenged. "You want to have more backbone and be more assertive? This is a good place to start."

She shook her head. "Inside I'm still a romantic," she confessed. "I might get to that point fairly soon, but it feels wrong to stand here and discuss going out because I need to be more assertive."

"I'm not willing to be a test subject either. But I have to suggest that, when this is over, maybe we should have dinner and see if there's something you want to pursue."

His wording caught her by surprise. "*Something I want to pursue?*"

He nodded. "Whether you feel like I am somebody you can trust, and you're willing to take another step, if you're even interested ... That means, you need to make a decision as to if it's something you wish to pursue."

"That doesn't sound very romantic," she declared.

He stared at her for a long moment. "How about this then?" He drew her gently toward him, slowly giving her a chance to pull away, lowered his head until he was just above her lips and whispered, "You have to let me know if you'll trust me after this." And he kissed her.

Her knees sagged, and her heart raced as he completely annihilated any and all resistance and showed her what passion truly was. A spark somewhere deep inside her belly surged up her stomach, to her ribs and exploded as she responded to his kiss. She threw her arms around his neck and plastered herself against his body.

He wrapped his arms tightly around her and crushed her against him. It was impossible to ignore the ridge nestled against her groin. And all she wanted to do was knock him flat and explore him in greater detail.

Shocked at her own response, and yet completely incapable of stepping back, she was lost when he lifted his head and deliberately placed her back a step out of his arms. She murmured in protest.

He shook his head. "You are deadly," he muttered, his breathing uneven. "If this is what you were like with Carlos, no way in hell that man went to something better. Maybe you were too much for him."

As much as she'd like to think that Liam could be right, she couldn't let him continue with that misunderstanding. But it was hard to get her breathing under control enough that she could speak. When she finally could, she took a deep breath and slowly let it out. "No," she said, "it wasn't like that with Carlos."

A light came on in his huge chocolate-colored eyes.

"Good," he murmured. He lifted a hand, cupping her chin and cheek, his thumb gently stroking her lips. "Because I'm totally okay if that's kept under wraps just for me." He leaned forward and kissed her hard. "But we've got really crappy timing."

She gave a happy sigh and nodded. "Isn't that the truth? I suppose North is watching us, isn't he?"

"If he saw us, he'd be a gentleman and not say anything," Liam said. "And he would never stand there and watch." He wrapped an arm around her shoulders and tugged her a little closer. "And now that we have that settled, and we'll pursue a relationship when this is over with, let's go in and see what kind of damage your sister has done."

"It's so hard to accept. I keep hoping there's a misunderstanding and she's innocent, but …"

"So do I," Liam said. "But let's not live in fantasy land while reality turns around and bites us in the ass."

His wording was a little too appropriate, given what she'd apparently not seen happening around her up until now. She stepped in through the open French doors of the office to see North standing in front of the open safe.

She looked up at him. "How did you open that?"

Liam stepped in. "Your father sent us the combination to the lock. But I have to be honest and say, both of us could have opened it regardless."

She gave them each a startled look. "Safecrackers?"

"Good at our jobs," North said with a half grin. He nodded at the two of them. "Still not sure how come I never get the girl though."

At that she realized he'd seen them. Color washed over her face, and she looked at the carpet. But she couldn't avoid him forever. She looked up and said, "Next time."

188

But he was already pulling envelopes from the safe. "Is this your dad's stuff or is this Carlos's stuff? That's what we need to figure out." He opened one envelope, whistled and handed it to her.

She looked at it and cried out. "Oh, my God! This is all cash."

They pulled out the envelopes, realized there was ten of them, and each was fully filled with cash.

She looked at North. "Where's this money coming from?"

"At this point, we're not sure. For all we know, Carlos is doing some money laundering, or he's doing jobs he's getting paid cash for, and it's not going in any accounting ledgers. But a lot of money is here," North said. "We should let the lawyers know."

Liam nodded. "Do you want to call?"

North looked at the money and said, "What I don't want is to put all this back in the safe and have Carlos and your sister take it and run. There's enough money here to operate the sanctuary for a good two years."

She stared at the envelopes. "Make that five," she cried out. "How could anybody do this?"

He rested a hand on her shoulder. "Remember, Carlos was in business himself. This might not have anything to do with sanctuary money."

She tried to pull herself together, but to see that much cash in one place was hard. "Could this be the sanctuary's money? Or Dad's?"

"We're taking it just in case. If nothing else, it's collateral against money they might have taken that they weren't entitled to. The lawyers will work it out, but it could take some time to go through all the accounting and find out what's gone missing and where."

North walked out into the hall, already talking on his phone.

Liam looked at the safe. "I wonder if we can change the combination. It's an old-style manual one. There's got to be some way to do it, but I don't know how. If it was electronic, we could set a new password."

"Any way to close it so it can't be opened again?"

"Let's see if North knows once he's off the phone." Liam walked over to the desk and pulled out the bottom drawer. "Come and take a look at this." He motioned at the drawer.

She walked over and saw more cash, her heart almost stopping at the sheer mass of it, and then she saw the handgun. She frowned. "I don't remember ever seeing one of those in the house."

"That's what I was wondering, if it was yours, your sister's or Carlos's."

North came back in again. "The property is her father's. There's no agreement with Brianna or Carlos. The lawyers suggested we remove the money, bring it to town so it goes into a safe-deposit box, lock up the safe and leave everything else here as it is." He turned to look at Lilianna. "Your father wants to know if his personal belongings are here."

She took a deep breath. "We'll go see." She looked at the money in the desk drawer. "I'm not comfortable leaving any of this here."

"We'll take what's in the safe. It is by rights your father's property," North said. "But the stuff in the drawer, I'm afraid if we take that, it'll trigger somebody to look for more money in the safe. Still I'm not comfortable leaving it."

"I agree," North said.

"Good. Me too." She nodded. "You want to collect that

and get it out to the truck and then pick us up?"

He considered that and nodded. "I can do that."

Lilianna walked into the kitchen, found a tall brown-paper grocery bag in one of the drawers and brought it to the office where she handed it over to North.

North packed up all the envelopes from the safe, then emptied the cash from the drawer and walked out the double French doors.

After he left, Liam closed the safe, returned the picture in front of it, locked the French doors and said, "Let's go find the rest of your father's belongings."

HE WATCHED THE determination in her face. The money had been a huge eye-opener. "We have to understand that the money could have been Carlos's."

"Good. I hope it is. Then he can explain to the tax man how he got it and how much tax he's paid on it," she said in a curt tone.

He grinned. "That'll bite. If it's cash, chances are it's under the table."

"Exactly." She quickly did a circle through the other bedrooms to make sure nothing of her father's was there, stopped in front of her closet, opened it up and saw just bedding and towels. She raced downstairs to the first floor, and he followed. She walked to a small doorway, opened it, clicked on the lights and headed into a basement.

It was unusual to have a basement in most places in Texas. Liam hadn't been prepared to look for one either. Once in the basement, he realized it was more of a crawl space. An access location for all the utilities running in the house. Lilianna crouched down and, with the lights on, took a good look around. She turned to him. "Not even one box, one sack, one piece of anything is down here."

She made her way back to the living room and stared at the furniture. "This is still the same furniture, but where are all my father's belongings?"

"Goodwill, I suspect," Liam said firmly. "They thought or planned that he would never come home again."

He heard her let out a small cry, then willed herself to be strong. He grabbed her fingers and said, "Remember? We're fixing this."

She nodded. She pulled out her phone and dialed Harry, her new lawyer. When he answered, she said, "May I talk to my father please?"

A moment later Liam heard her almost distressed voice.

"Dad, I can't find anything. Brianna and Carlos have moved into the master bedroom. All your stuff appears to have been cleaned out. The same furniture is here. The kitchen looks the same. But none of your clothing is here."

"Or any of his paperwork in the office that I can tell," Liam interrupted.

She turned to look at him. "Liam says he hasn't seen anything of yours in what's now Carlos's office either. I have to go back to the main tourist office for another look. We kept all the business papers there, but I didn't see anything the first time I went in. I don't know what you had in your office or in the rest of the house."

Liam watched as she nodded her head.

"He's asking if you've gotten into the big filing cabinet."

"It's locked," Liam said. "If he wants me to check inside, I'll break in if he can't tell me where the key is."

She explained that to her father, then turned to look at Liam, a hard glint in her eye. "Dad says it was never locked."

Liam raised his eyebrows and headed back for the office. He stood in front of the three-drawer file cabinet. It was just a simple metal one. He pulled out his tools, and, within seconds, he had picked the lock. He opened the top drawer. It was full of files. He opened the second one and the third one. The top one appeared to be the most current. He pulled it out again and stepped aside for Lilianna to read off the labels to see if any of it made any sense to her father.

"What do we do with it all?" she asked her father.

Liam heard a truck. He walked out to the front entry-way, checking who it was through a window, relieved to see it was North. Motioned for him to come on in.

North walked in the front door and said, "Anything else we're taking?"

Liam returned to the home office. "Does your father want these? They could all belong to Carlos."

"He wants all the files." She looked around and pointed to several discarded banker's boxes off on the side, lying at odd angles and obviously empty. "We're to take everything we can."

Liam nodded. "What about from the sanctuary office?" He only half listened as he packed up the complete contents of the filing cabinet. Thankfully there were enough banker's boxes to empty it out. Then he walked over to the desk and pointed at the file drawers here.

This time she had no hesitation. "Pack it all up. They can go through their lawyers to get any of this back, if and when any of it's allowed to return to them."

He nodded. "Good enough for me." He needed to give Levi an update. *As soon as we get out of here.* It took them fifteen minutes to pack up the remaining files.

With all the files loaded into the bed of the truck, they

still had to hit the sanctuary office again, and they wanted to get off the property before anybody came back. He walked back inside and saw her standing there. "Are you okay?"

She nodded. "I am, but at the same time I'm not."

"Understood. We're all set here, but I'm worried we missed something in the business office."

She nodded. "Let's head down there and see."

Outside, she closed the door but left it unlocked as she always had. She motioned at the truck. "I'll walk down with the dogs."

Liam nodded. "I'll come with you." He gave a hard pat on the truck to let North know he could carry on.

North turned on the vehicle and slowly drove it to the office. With the two dogs joining them, tails wagging furiously, Lilianna and Liam walked in the back door of the tourist building to see Daniel pouring coffee.

"Hey, what's going on?" he asked. "Sounds like something's up."

She grinned and said, "The best thing of all is up."

"What's that?"

She couldn't keep the grin off her face, and Liam loved to watch her light up like a candle as she spoke.

"My father. He's back to normal, and he's returning home tomorrow or the next day."

Chapter 12

LILIANNA'S FACE TOOK on a complete look of joy. As far as Liam could see, it was natural.

Daniel grabbed her in a great big hug and twirled her around the room. "Are you serious? The new medication worked?"

"Actually he's off all medications now."

"Fantastic. I know he was given something months ago. I was hoping that it would work, but it seems like he's been gone for so long."

"Well, he's back now," she said, teary-eyed. "He's staying with a friend for a couple days while he regains some strength, and we'll grab some of the files from the office here to bring him up to date on what we've done for the last couple years."

Daniel nodded. "That's a good idea," he said. "Everything should be digital anyway, right? So take the laptop too. And, if you've got any paper files, maybe just scan them all in right now, take the paper copies with you. Then, if anything happens, we still have the digitals."

She stopped, struck by the sense of that. "That's what we always used to do, isn't it?"

"Yeah, but, once Brianna took over in the office, she stopped doing it that way." He walked with her to the back office, opening a closet door and pointing out the boxes of folders. "I hadn't realized how much paperwork is here. It will take hours to digitize all this."

She shook her head, raising both hands in frustration. "If you do it at the time, it only takes a few minutes."

"I know."

"I don't think I have time right now. And Dad wants to see everything."

"Well, everything should have been entered into ledgers in the accounting system," Daniel said. "So, in theory, it should all be online." His voice was doubtful.

"What we can do," Liam said, "is take in the originals. There should be a scanning company in town. We'll drop the boxes off and get them all digitally scanned while we have lunch and talk to your father. We should be able to get them all back here again before long."

She frowned. "But it'll still take hours."

Daniel was already opening one box, frowning. "This one's almost empty." He pulled out the stacks. "I can feed this through right now. He walked over to the scanner, placed in the papers. He pushed the Scan button and ran them through.

While he was doing that, Lilianna opened up the next box. She looked at Liam. "Do you think we have an hour?"

He frowned, considering the option.

"I don't have a whole lot of choice. We could take it to town, but I think it's safer and easier if done here."

He nodded. "While Daniel scans this stuff, you go through the desk and see if there's anything else your father wants."

Switching places, Lilianna sat down at the desk to read through the files while Daniel continued to shove stacks of paper through the scanner. Liam was right though. They needed to get this done.

"If you don't mind me asking, what's the panic?" Daniel asked.

"My sister. I think she's pulling a fast one on the sanctuary."

"Do you know anything about that?" Liam asked.

Daniel shrugged. "She's my boss, and I can't really say anything bad against her."

"If she's stealing from the sanctuary you can," Liam said, crossing his arms over his chest. "And she very well could be."

Daniel hesitated for just one second, then nodded. "You know that almost makes sense. She kept telling us there was no money, no money, and yet it seemed like there was lots of money the last time I looked at the accounts. Next time it was empty and never refilled again. And then I was locked out about a month ago. She told me that she was keeping a tighter grip on the account in case somebody was helping themselves." He gave Lilianna a resentful look. "At the time I was pretty upset, like she was accusing me, but, when she gave me access again, I didn't think anything about it anymore."

She shook her head. "I'm so sorry. That's such a Brianna thing to do, throwing the blame on somebody else."

"She did say you were taking your expenses and how you refused to take a pay cut," he admitted.

Lilianna's jaw dropped. "Seriously?"

He nodded. "Yeah, that's what she said."

"I take $500 a month for all the traveling I do."

He stared at her. "That's not even a wage."

"No. But I understood no money was left, and I couldn't figure out why."

At that Daniel didn't say anything.

"I think you both know why," Liam said.

Daniel said, "I've downloaded the last year's accounting, but I need something to copy it to."

Liam stepped forward and gave him a USB key, stood over his shoulder to make sure it downloaded. As soon as it was, Daniel pulled out the key and gave it back.

Lilianna nodded. "You're the one who always brought us back when we got into trouble."

"I'm not just a pretty face," Daniel joked.

When he was done, he stood and said, "Now Brianna can still see what's there, but you can too. You have access to all the emails running through the sanctuary."

"Okay, I've got my laptop. We're taking all the paperwork. I still have one box to scan." She stared at it with a frown.

"If you want, you guys can take off. I'll scan all this stuff in. You should be able to access all the digital files from your laptops."

"Sure, but I kind of want the paper copies too." She looked up as Liam walked back in and snatched another box of scanned paperwork and left. "Let's just do this now."

It took another fifteen minutes to get through the stacks. She was glad she had picked up a decent printer/scanner that could go through the pages at such a fast rate.

Finally they had them all scanned. She gave the last box to Liam, telling him, "There's still more stuff here. I just want to make sure, if this place burns to the ground, I have everything I need to stay in business."

Daniel froze, then exclaimed, "Is that likely?"

She shrugged. "I don't know. I'm afraid of what could happen."

Liam heard her. "That's a good point." He tapped his foot thoughtfully and pulled out his phone, calling Levi. "Levi, we might need some men here. To make sure nothing happens to the structures on the property. There's the office, the big house, Lilianna's cabin and the barn for the elephants. Not to mention all the elephant-proof fencing. The last thing I want is to have a fire here. If any one of the bad guys finds out what we've taken, there's no telling what they'll do."

Lilianna stared at him, her mind filling with thoughts of what somebody who was angry could do to this sanctuary. She shook her head. "Jesus Christ! If that's the case, I'm not leaving."

Daniel reached out a hand. "Go. I don't know what you're up to, but I presume it's important, and it has to do with keeping this place safe."

She nodded. "It does indeed. We're caught up in legal battles to stop Brianna and Carlos from getting their hands on the sanctuary."

Daniel nodded. "That's what I thought. Look. I'll stay, and I'm sure I can grab the other two local guys and see if they'll pull an all-nighter here with me."

"Sure," Lilianna said, "but what will you do if Carlos and Brianna come back? I also can't be sure they won't come back alone."

Just then Liam said, "Levi is sending over four men." He turned to look at Daniel. "If you're willing to stay, those four will stand watch."

"Are they the unarmed bodyguard type?" Daniel asked in a hard tone. "Because, if we're talking about someone torching the elephant barn, I won't tolerate that. I've got two rifles here on the property. I'm not afraid to use them."

She watched as Liam eyed Daniel with an equally hard look. And then Liam nodded. "All four will be armed. They can be very dangerous. But they'll be on your side."

She could see the relief on Daniel's face. He was a good man. He'd been there every step of the way. But he wasn't a warrior until pushed to defend. He was the kind of man who healed.

"Maybe we should move the elephants to another pasture," she said quietly. "Keep them away from the barn for now."

Daniel thought about that for a moment, walked to the map and pointed to an area. "I presume the problem is this lovely lake area again?"

"Oh, it so is," she confirmed. "But we need the water rights off that lake for the elephants."

He nodded. "I'll put them in this area. Moses and Joshua should be there now."

She stood beside him at the map. "So it's a matter of getting Billie, Mandy and Sally over there."

"That's easy. I've got another load of watermelons to feed them. I'll load up a four-wheeler and the trailer. They'll follow me if I have watermelons."

"If you could do that now, that would be perfect. I'll get back here as soon as I can."

Liam interrupted. "I've got a worrisome inkling that we need to hurry up this process a bit. We should help you load up the four-wheeler, so we make sure the elephants are out of the barn before we leave the property."

Lilianna bobbed her head in agreement. "I know I'd feel better seeing them heading off."

Daniel nodded too. About fifteen minutes later, with the trailer full of watermelons, Daniel shared his thanks with

Liam and Lilianna. As she was about to leave, Daniel called back to her, "Hey, you take care yourself. I don't need to know what the hell is going on, but, just for the record, Carlos has never been friendly or willing to give an inch." Daniel stopped, hesitated, then added, "You know your sister will never, ever let you win."

Lilianna smiled. "She doesn't have to *let* me win. I just have to make sure she loses." She turned and walked out, calling for the dogs. No way was she leaving them behind. Not when things were looking to get even uglier. Gunner would keep them for her until this was settled one way or the other.

THEY WERE TEN minutes into the trip back to Gunner's when Liam, his instincts pricking at him, looked at North and said, "I wonder how quickly Levi's men are coming. I have a bad feeling about this."

"Me too," North said. "I don't like the idea of leaving the place unattended."

Lilianna snorted. "I've been saying that since the beginning," she said from the back seat.

"I know. I'll find out where they are." Liam pulled out his cell phone and called Levi. "What's the ETA on the men?"

"They should be there in about fifteen minutes."

Liam nodded. "Okay, we're about ten minutes away from the property. We were heading to Gunner's, but I'm getting a really ugly feeling."

"Can you turn back?" Levi asked.

There was never any questioning that sense of foreboding in their line of work, especially coming from their navy roots. When somebody said they had an ugly feeling, everybody jumped in to do what they could.

"We could, but we're carrying a lot of money and all the paper financial documents." There was an indrawn breath from the other end of his phone, and Liam understood how Levi felt. "If the guys are coming in a SUV, I could ride back with them, and North and Lilianna could go on to Gunner's with all the boxes of cash and financials."

"That might not be a bad idea," Levi admitted. "How intense is the feeling?"

"Strong and getting worse." He grabbed North's shoulder. "Pull over."

Levi's voice was sharp, "That bad?"

"Hell, yeah. Call the men. Tell them that I'm on the side of the road, the same side they're heading, and to pick me up." He hung up. As North pulled off to the side, Liam said, "Get her out of here. Get all this documentation and the money out of here." He jumped out, slammed the door, pounded hard on the truck to make sure North took off fast because he knew, in his heart of hearts, Lilianna would try to get out with him.

Sure enough, she called out, "What are you doing?"

He could hardly hear her over the dogs barking. He just waved her on. "Go," he said.

And North gunned it back onto the highway. She was still screaming, "No," in the distance.

The highway was pretty well empty. He crossed the road and ran alongside it, not able to stand still, too pumped up with adrenaline to just wait passively. The four men should be here within a few minutes. He didn't know if he'd know who they were or not, but he'd take anybody right now. Any one of his unit would be a good deal. As long as North got

Lilianna away from here so Liam knew she would be safe, then he didn't have to worry about that.

It wasn't dark yet, but the running lights of an oncoming truck bore down on him. He held up a hand and waved. He wasn't sure who it was, but, if they stopped, he figured they had been expecting to see him. In fact, there were two trucks. They both pulled to the shoulder. He got in the back seat of the second one and smiled at Harrison and Logan in the front seat. "Glad to see you guys. Now drive…"

"What the hell's going on?" Logan asked, his tone worried as the truck pulled back onto the highway. "Where is Lilianna? Is she okay?"

There was more than caring in his voice, and it stopped Liam in his thoughts. "She's fine," he said slowly. "Did you two have a thing in the past?"

Logan shook his head. "No, but she was always so damn quiet, so sweet compared to the rest of the nightmarish women in that family. It was hard not to be nice to her. She's kind of like a kid sister."

Liam nodded. "I can't say I feel the kid-sister thing at all, but she's definitely a sweetheart."

Logan shot him a look and then chuckled. "Wow. I should've seen that one coming."

"North said something strange. He wondered how come it's never his turn, and I just had to laugh because there was no warning, and suddenly Lilianna was right there in front of me. Only that's changed. I need to make damn sure she's okay."

Logan nodded. "It happens that way sometimes."

Harrison outright laughed. "With our group, it always happens that way. … Nothing, nothing and *bam*! There's two of you where there used to only be one."

"Any regrets?" Liam asked. "I'm just wondering how and if the efforts are worth it."

"Absolutely it's worth it. I think the danger of our assignment accelerates the relationship, making things happen faster, easier, because you get to the core of what is really important. And, if things have heated up between you really fast, that's just following the same pattern as all the rest of us."

Logan got them back to the more urgent matter at hand. "We've got Flynn and Rhodes in the other vehicle. So fill us in on what's going on."

Liam told them about the money they found in the safe, the handgun with more money, the files they'd digitized and what had happened to her father.

Logan was pissed when he heard that. "Jesus! Jim is an awesome guy. I was so upset when I found out what happened. Dad was absolutely devastated for days."

"And it might all have been for naught," Liam said. "As you know, he's back to normal now, or maybe you don't know. But he's at your dad's house, recuperating. We got him out of that assisted-care home real fast. The specialist your father brought in and Gunner's lawyer are looking after Jim right now."

Logan nodded. "If Dad is on the case, things will move forward quickly."

As they drove around a corner, Liam saw flames coming up over the rise. "Jesus Christ," he roared. "That's her place."

Harrison said, "Do you know what building that is? Are there any animals around it?"

"It's Lilianna's cabin," Liam almost yelled. "She's got the dogs with her, thank God." The truck raced up the hill toward her cabin, stopping a decent distance away. It was too late to save anything. "We haven't even been gone twenty minutes," he roared.

"Either somebody came in behind you, or somebody was already there and waited for you to leave."

Harrison got out of the truck. The other vehicle pulled up behind them. A man raced toward them from the other side of the cabin. It was Daniel. His face was covered in soot; his clothing was covered in dirt.

When he saw Liam, he cried out, "I got hit from behind. When I woke up it was already on fire."

"Do you have any big equipment here?" Harrison asked desperately. "A tractor, something to make a dirt boundary to stop the fire from spreading?"

Daniel nodded. "Yes, this way."

The two men raced off. There wasn't much the others could do but stand and watch and wait.

"Are we expecting anybody to set one of the other buildings on fire?" Logan asked.

"It could happen." Liam's voice was hard, angry. "I don't trust anybody at this place anymore. There's no way to know. I don't know who the hell lit this fire."

Rhodes was with Flynn as they stepped up. Flynn asked, "Do you think Daniel had anything to do with it?"

Liam raised his hands. "Honest to God, I don't know the man."

"Her mom's quite the bitch," Logan said suddenly. "Do we know where the hell she's at?"

Liam spun to look at him. "No clue."

"You're not missing much if you've never met her," Logan said.

Just then the sound of a tractor came up the hill. Daniel drove, Harrison standing on the back. The tractor had forks on the front and a bucket-loader with teeth on the back.

All they could do at this point was set up a dirt guard about twenty feet from the cabin to stop the fire from spreading to the trees or the grass. The cabin would burn to the ground. There wasn't anything anybody could do about it.

"That's the original worker's cabin on the property," Logan said. "Her father won't be happy about this. The problem is, it could be the main house next." He turned to look around, but Rhodes and Flynn had all spread out, each taking up a spot to watch the other buildings from. "The elephant barn is the most worrisome. We can always rebuild a house. But it takes a lot of money to get another barn like that built."

Knowing that the cabin was gone, and Daniel and Harrison were tending to the fire while Rhodes and Flynn were keeping watch on the inhabited parts of the property, Liam and Logan ran toward the elephant barn. Almost instantly Liam could smell gas. He called Harrison on the phone. "There is gas all around the elephant barn. Bring the tractor," he cried.

Just then a figure ran from the barn up to the far side. Logan dashed after him.

Liam found water spigots on the outside of the barn and doused the gasoline to thin it down. It could still burn. If they could soak it enough though, whoever would try to light it couldn't make it go up. He saw Daniel and Harrison bringing the tractor as fast as it could trundle toward them.

Harrison was driving now—probably a good idea with the hit to the head Daniel just received—and plowed back the dirt around the barn and the entranceway. These buildings were mostly metal, but, if hay was inside, and feed and sawdust in the stalls, it would be a nightmare. Liam was so glad he and Lilianna had helped Daniel move the animals out of the barn earlier before someone decked him.

Liam entered the barn and looked around. Without any animals, it looked like a skeleton cage set to hold some kind of prehistoric dinosaurs, it was so vast. It was amazing just how much space the elephants needed. But what he had to do now was make sure nobody else tried to set this place on fire. He sent out a wild bird call, hoping Logan would hear him. There was an answer off to the left. Liam wondered if that meant whoever Logan was chasing was still nearby. Liam slid to his side, crouching beside the hay bales. He dove in beside Logan.

"Somebody is on the far side."

Liam nodded. "I'm going after him. The last thing we want is for someone to toss a match in here."

"You go left. I'll go right," Logan said.

They jumped to their feet. Liam could only hope nobody had a weapon. Of course, it was Texas, and they all had guns.

The first shot rang out as a warning over his head. But instead of going down, he picked up his speed, and, instead of running around the hay—he judged the depth to be too deep—with direct propulsion, he plowed into the top two bales, sending them flying over the side. A woman's voice cried out, and he jumped over the last of the tumbling bales and landed near her.

She had a lighter in her hand. She grinned. "Go ahead. I'll drop this, and the place will go up in flames."

Liam studied her. "I guess you're the ex-wife and the mother then, huh?"

She raised an elegantly trimmed eyebrow and said, "Of

course."

"So how did your son die?"

Here face twisted in fury. "None of your business."

He nodded with a sad smile. "Lilianna will have a hard time when she finds out you killed her brother, your own son. Why did you do it? To hurt Jim?"

Like watching her face disintegrate, this previously calm woman holding a lighter in her hand became a raving maniac, screaming and shouting obscenities about Keith.

Until Logan stepped up behind her and clipped her hard on the side of the head.

She dropped the lighter, which closed and fell harmlessly to the floor.

Liam stared down at her. "What the hell was that?"

"That was Jim's nightmare of a wife," Logan said. "He couldn't get rid of her fast enough, but she was somebody who wouldn't stay gone."

"And she killed her own son to hurt her ex?"

"I don't know the details," Logan said. "But he died in a fire, I do know that."

As they looked at the damage she had caused today, Liam said, "She does appear to have a firebug issue—someone definitely needs to check deeper into her son's death."

Logan grabbed a lasso from the barn wall, rolled her over, tied her wrists behind her back, and then wrapped the rope tightly around her legs, looping the end back into the ropes at her wrists, a typical hog-tie maneuver.

"Check her for weapons too," Liam said. "That bitch is somebody you can't trust in any way."

Logan nodded. "She's packing a handgun, I believe. Check her pants at the waistband."

Liam found it and pulled out an ankle holster revolver as well. "Do you think it's safe now? Was she working alone?"

"I don't know," Logan said, "but we haven't seen anyone else. I presume we saw her running away earlier. We are limited on manpower, but I can send out Harrison, once he's finished digging a ditch around the barn, and maybe take Flynn off guard duty, now that the cabin and the barn are dealt with as much as we can do right now. As a two-man team, they can check the public lands in the front of the property to make sure."

"How did she get here? There's no vehicle. She doesn't look like the kind of woman to walk very far." He kicked the heeled boots she wore. "These won't go very far either."

Several men gathered around. Daniel introduced the two newcomers to Liam as their local hired help. Daniel took one look down at their feet and cried out, "Oh, my God! She's back?"

"Did you see a vehicle?" Liam said.

Daniel nodded. "I thought I heard one up on the hill. But, with the tractor going, I couldn't be sure. I saw the lights and went to look because there shouldn't have been a vehicle there."

The tractor was working hard out front, making sure the residue of gasoline couldn't cause further harm. Harrison was still dragging a burn-resistant pathway up and around the elephant barn.

Liam looked at Daniel and said, "Show me."

Logan joined them long enough to say he was going for the truck to traverse the property as fast as they could. He left the sad excuse for a mother on the barn floor with a warning to the two local employees to make sure, if she regained consciousness, to clip her a healthy one so she went out again.

Once they made it to the back of the property, they found an SUV with four-wheel drive. But the tracks leading to it didn't come from the established ranch road. They came from the direction of the trees on the left.

"What do you want to bet someone has built a basic road from the lake?" Logan asked.

Liam walked over to the vehicle, opened it and checked out the registration. "Look at that. Her name is Rianna." He shook his head. "Lilianna, Brianna and Rianna. How bloody typical."

"Right?" In the back of the SUV they found several five-gallon gas cans and even more small propane bottles. They looked at each other with grim faces. "She came prepared."

"Is this a case of, *if she can't have it, nobody can?*"

"Did she hurt the elephants though?" Daniel cried out. "I have to check them. I moved them over to the far side, but that could be where the road is coming through from the development area."

"Chances are she didn't because the elephants were bringing in money. But we do need to check on them."

Logan said, "I'll bring my truck closer."

They stood here, waiting, searching the SUV for anything else they might find. Rianna's purse was here and her cell phone. Liam turned on the phone and pocketed it when he found it locked. He also picked up her purse, so she couldn't grab it if she managed to get free. Nothing else of any value was in the vehicle.

With Logan driving toward them, Liam and Daniel jumped in the bed of the truck, and they took off toward the elephants. By now, dusk had settled in, but the night sky was lit bright from the cabin fire still raging on the side hill. But it was down to a simple heavy burn that hopefully wouldn't go anywhere. Flynn, Harrison and Rhodes would continue to keep an eye on all of it.

They were a good twenty minutes driving across land, following the tracks Rianna had used to get into the place, when Daniel said, "Stop over there." He hopped out, walked over to a big secured gate. He crawled through the fence and walked a few feet, calling, "Mandy! Billie! Where are you?"

Soon there was a heavy rumbling and an elephant cry in the night. Logan and Liam hopped out of the vehicle and walked into the fenced area to stand at Daniel's side. A big female elephant walked toward them. Daniel reached up his arms when she got close, and she wrapped her trunk around him, hugging him close. Daniel scratched her face.

"Mandy, there you are, girl. I'm hoping everything's okay. Where are the others?"

Mandy lowered to one knee, and Daniel hopped up. "She's the only one that we can ride," he said with a big grin.

Logan said, "I'll ride a horse but not an elephant. Let's take a walk, and make sure the others are okay."

Slowly they moved at her side toward where the other elephants were. Liam marveled at the grace and beauty of the huge animal at his side. Mandy appeared to be completely content. As they came over yet another rolling rise, they found the other elephants waiting for them.

Daniel called out, "All five are here."

And suddenly Liam was completely surrounded by elephant trunks, sniffing his jacket, his face, his hair.

Daniel explained, "They're just checking you out."

Liam stood quietly and let them. He reached up to pat trunks and faces, scratched the sides of heads and ears.

"Do we have anything to feed them?" Logan said.

"I've got watermelons back at the barn, but they've pretty well eaten everything I gave them earlier. We'll have more to give them tomorrow. But not tonight."

"Good enough as long as they're all safe."

"I think it's safe to call it a night. … Or maybe not."

Another vehicle's headlights shone in the darkening area. They walked to meet the truck. Two doors slammed shut, and a female voice called out, "Daniel?"

It was Lilianna. North at her side.

Daniel called back, "They're all fine, Lilianna."

"Oh, thank God," she cried as she raced toward them, her hands reaching up to stroke and cuddle the animals. She was evidently a favorite as all their trunks wrapped around her, touching, caressing, nibbling. She laughed. "We'll have to come back in the morning with the rest of the watermelons."

"I know, right?" Daniel said. "For now we need to make sure the cabin fire didn't spread."

Lilianna turned her gaze, looking from one man to the other, landing on Liam.

"You," she cried out. She walked over, hauled back and smacked him hard across the face. Then with both hands she pushed against his chest, sending him back one step at the unexpected move. "Don't you dare do that again. Don't you realize you could've been hurt? You had no business leaving me with North." Then, as if giving up all her temper, she threw her arms around his neck and kissed him hard.

Liam went from experiencing shock to amusement to passion in a heartbeat. He wrapped his arms around her and kissed her back hungrily.

Chapter 13

I T WAS HARD to explain the panic in her heart when Lilianna had urged North to drive faster and faster up the driveway. Her father and Gunner were behind them in Gunner's vehicle. They'd gone to Gunner's, dropped off the boxes and money and electronics, brought the men up to speed and raced back out again.

When she'd seen her cabin in flames, she'd been so damn terrified somebody would get hurt. Of course, it was the old cabin, *her place*, that would have gone down first. It was sad, but it wasn't the heartbreaking loss of a person or an elephant.

Regardless she'd loved the cabin, and it had been a place to call home, but it had been literally one of the oldest buildings on the property. But to see the elephants, to know they were safe, to know Daniel was safe, and then to finally realize Liam too was safe, she'd just lost it—as if something had snapped inside—and she was all over him. She must have looked like a fool. But, at the moment, she couldn't stop kissing him.

His hands gently eased up and down her back, and then he just held her tight against him.

She could feel the tremors rocking through her, but she no longer knew if they were passion or fear. She'd been so damn scared.

He continued to hold her close until she calmed down.

She recognized the sound of another truck arriving and could hear the other voices around them. New voices joining them. She looked up to see Gunner's truck. Gunner and her father, plus three more men she didn't know now surrounded them. Well, four men she didn't know, eyeing the guy who had been here already with Liam and Daniel.

Liam whispered in her ear, "That's Flynn, Harrison and Rhodes who also work with me at Levi's place. Plus Logan's here." Liam pointed to him.

Daniel took one look at Jim and reached out with a hand. "Damn, do you look good."

Her father grinned and shook his hand. "I am so damn sorry, Daniel."

Daniel shook his head. "No. Don't be. Just make sure you're back this time. I don't want to go through again what we've been through these last couple years."

"Neither do I." Her father walked up to the elephants.

Billie walked over and wrapped her trunk around Jim. He stood in her embrace, his arms wrapped around her trunk and held on for dear life.

Gunner stood next to Liam and Lilianna. "I figured this was about the best healing he could get."

She smiled, tears in her eyes as she watched her father spend time greeting each of the elephants individually. They knew him and had missed him just as much as everyone else. When Jim returned to join them, he was brushing tears from his eyes. "I can't believe I've lost two years of this," he muttered. "I still don't understand all of what happened."

"Did you stop at the barn before you came up?" Liam asked.

"The men said you were up here. We came straightaway."

Logan looked over at Liam who looked down at Lilianna. And then he looked at her father. "I think it's your ex-wife, Rianna. She's tied up in the barn. Your two local employees are standing by."

"Tied up?" Lilianna stepped out of Liam's embrace. "Why?"

"Because she was trying to burn down the barn," he said in a hard voice. "And she most likely is the one who lit the fire to your cabin."

She stared up at him wordlessly. How could she possibly even begin to process this? She turned to look back at her father. He looked shell-shocked but in a way not surprised. "Dad?"

He glanced at her, diverted his eyes and sighed heavily. "I always suspected she might have lit the fire that killed Keith."

Lilianna shook her head. "No. Why? Why would she do that?"

But her father couldn't—wouldn't answer.

It was Liam who said, "I would imagine because she couldn't get between Keith and your father. And it was also the best way to hurt your father."

Lilianna, her heart now wounded and aching at the thought, turned to stare at her father again. "Are you saying she did it on purpose?" She shook her head. "Please tell me that Keith wasn't killed over a mother's jealousy."

"It'll be a while before we can get the truth out of your mother," her father said. "But I highly suspect it was deliberate."

Lilianna turned toward her father. He opened his arms, and she raced into them. The two clung to each other like they should have done in the beginning. She gripped him hard, feeling the sobs shattering her inside. But her father was stronger than she was at the moment, and he just supported her.

She looked up at him. "Did you know?"

"No," he said. "But I suspected."

"Why didn't you say anything?" she cried out. "We could've had an investigation and caught her back then."

"I was too overwhelmed with grief. And despondent over her betrayal. Keith was special. I love you as much as I love him, but the bond he and I shared was there from his birth. And she hated it. She absolutely hated it. She always tried to do what she could to split us up, but I never thought she'd go so far as to kill him."

"We could also put an element of doubt in here," Gunner said. "It could be that she lit the hay on fire, not knowing Keith was working around it. Not knowing his clothes would catch fire, and it would kill him."

Her father took a deep breath. "Thank you, Gunner. I'll hang on to that for the moment."

Lilianna wasn't so sure she could. This was just too unbelievable and too damn painful. She returned to Liam and instinctively walked right back into his embrace. He held her close, and she knew he understood. Just too many damn shocks. She looked at Gunner. "Are we assuming she's behind all of this then?"

"Your sister and Carlos are being picked up right now," he said. "Once we realized the building was on fire, I brought the cops right back into it. It'll take time to sort out what's with the money and if they were into anything else criminal, but the cops will hold all three of them as suspects for now."

"For everything?"

He nodded. "*Everything.*"

She sighed and let her head rest against Liam's chest. "So, is it over then?"

Gunner nodded. "It's over."

"I should've come to you earlier, shouldn't I?"

A deep rumbling laugh came from Gunner. "It would have been good if you had but better late than never. I don't know about you guys, since you're all young, but I want to go home and have a real bed to sleep in for the night."

"I don't feel like we should leave this place just yet," Lilianna said. "I still want answers. It's hard to not know *why.*"

"*Why* is easy," Liam said. "Money." He shook his head. "It was all about the money."

"Lilianna, you can sleep in the main house," her father said. "Your sister won't be back tonight."

"Are we sure about that?" she asked.

"Obviously not until we've heard they've been picked up by the cops, but, considering they were at a hotel, it shouldn't be too much longer before we hear."

Just then Gunner's phone rang. He answered with, "Please tell me you have good news?" He nodded, turned to look at Lilianna and said, "They've got Brianna. No sign of Carlos."

She buried her face against Liam, and his arms tightened. She let out a heavy sigh. "The next few days will be absolutely shitty," she announced.

The others chuckled. "They will be bad," North said. "At least we know the animals are safe, the rest of the buildings are safe, and your father is back to being his normal self."

She beamed at him. "You are a half-full kind of guy."

He chuckled. "That's Liam. He's always that way."

She looked around at the men. "What happens now?"

Logan said, motioning at the men he'd arrived with, "We'll stand watch all night. Just to make sure there are no other shenanigans."

She nodded. "Dad, what are you up to?"

He sighed. "I'll go to the main house and take a look around."

Just then Liam's phone rang. He pulled it out and answered it. "I'll be right down." He pocketed his phone. "That was North. They just caught Carlos inside the house." He gave Lilianna a hard grin. "Guess what he was after?"

"Let's go," her father said. "I want to have a talk with him."

Fuming all the way to the main house, Lilianna walked up to where Carlos stood arrogant and tall in front of her. North at his side, Carlos was handcuffed and curled his lip at her.

"How could you steal from me? From my father? What kind of man are you?"

"A real one," he said snidely. "Not that you recognized it. You're nothing but a faded copy of your sister. She was very anxious to set plans in motion to move her life forward. A woman after my own heart. The damn elephants don't need all this land. There was enough after the sale for them and us. Your father went to pieces after his son died, and you went to pieces after Jim collapsed." Carlos gave a head shake—sending the long lock of dark hair she'd once thought sexy back into place.

"And my mother? Brianna takes after her. Was she in on this too?"

"Of course. Although I'd have been fine if she wasn't. She's not the most stable person. Any mother who can kill her own son …"

A cry of pain escaped her. "Did she really kill Keith?"

Carlos nodded. "Brianna is a little afraid of her, I think. But your mother knew the developer. It was her plan. She wanted to get away from this dust bowl."

Lilianna, hearing an odd sound, turned to see her father's shocked face, his mouth working but nothing coming out.

She went to his side. "You don't have to do this now. It's enough we know the truth." She turned back to Carlos, even as her arms went around her father. "Where did the money come from?"

His face turned ugly. He stepped forward, but North jerked him back.

Liam stepped in. "Oh, no you don't."

Carlos glared at him. "So Lilianna finally found herself another lover. You must be desperate."

In a smooth move, Liam decked him. Carlos fell backward until North straightened him upright, holding him for Liam to take a second shot.

Carlos swore, his voice getting louder and louder.

Liam waited, his face implacable.

Lilianna had to admit, she was impressed. Carlos always seemed to be the one in control. Only Liam had him running his mouth off. She grinned. "What's the matter, Carlos? Up against a *real* man for once?" she taunted. "Don't look so good now, do you?" She couldn't help herself; she laughed at Carlos. "For stealing from the sanctuary, for trying to ruin the charity, sabotaging the website… I hope they lock you up and throw away the key. You're a taker in this world that's desperately in need of givers."

"That money you stole is mine. Your sister is the one who stole from the sanctuary. I came to collect my money. But you got here ahead of me, bitch."

"Resorting to name-calling now, are you?"

"Bitch, there's only winners and losers," he spat out.

Liam gave Carlos another taste of his fist.

Even with North's help, Carlos didn't seem as able to stay upright this time.

"And," he said, spitting out blood, "you'll never be anything other than a blander copy of your sister."

"Well, *this* sister," she snapped, "will be living free and clear and enjoying life at large while you and the other women in my family spend a lot of years contemplating your navels."

Her father's arms clutched her tight. She smiled at him, so glad to have him back here. Where he belonged. But maybe not for tonight. "Come on. Time for you to leave."

He shook his head. "No, we have too much to sort out."

"Tomorrow," Gunner said firmly. "We're going home. We'll have a good night's sleep. We'll get up in the morning. We'll have a good breakfast. Then we'll come back here and pick up the pieces."

Her father looked like he wanted to protest, but Gunner wasn't having anything to do with it. He grabbed his friend's arm and said, "Come on. Back to the truck with you. There are beds calling our names."

Within a few minutes the truck with the two of them inside slowly traveled down the road toward the highway.

"Daniel," Lilianna asked, "are you okay?"

"I'll be fine," he said. "Your mother must have hit me over the head and knocked me out. I have to admit, I'm looking forward to some sleep myself."

"Go. Take tomorrow off," she said, "and make sure you get that head looked after."

He chuckled. "I will." He walked back down the hill.

Harrison said, "Come on. Hop in, and I'll take you back to your vehicle."

Lilianna looked at the rest of the men. "North, what are you up to?"

"While I figure three spare bedrooms are in the main house, one of them might just be for me."

She nodded. "There absolutely is one for you."

With that settled, the four of them walked to the house. "Logan, are you and the rest of your team staying?"

"Hell yes," he said. "We'll make sure that fire doesn't go out of control."

"Will it burn all night?" she asked, casting a look at where her cabin still smoldered.

"It will. In the morning, if it's out, we'll take that tractor and spread the ashes around so we don't have to worry about it erupting again."

"If you want to put on coffee or avail yourself of any of the food in the house, please do."

"I'll come and make a pot of coffee right now," he said. "The guys will need it to stay awake as we take shifts tonight."

"There's probably marshmallows somewhere too," she said, her sad attempt at humor.

He chuckled. "I might not say no. There'll be a lot of good coals coming up."

Walking back into the house was a sad and eerie feeling. It didn't feel like her home. But once her father returned in the morning, she knew things would improve tremendously.

She was too damn tired to worry about it now that everything was basically over, and her father was safe now, and Liam was safe, and the animals were all fine. She was just way too damn exhausted to deal with anything else.

It was like the stuffing had been ripped out of her, and she had nothing left. She walked through the main house, showing Logan where he needed to get stuff, and then she headed upstairs. North walked into the bedroom at the front of the house, and she stopped, looking at the master bedroom where her sister and Carlos had been. No way she would sleep in there, and, by rights, it was her father's room. She headed instinctively back to the room she'd always been in. It was on the opposite side of the house.

As she walked in, she saw Liam's back as he stood at the window. "Oh. You'll be in this one. I will go to the other one," she said apologetically.

He turned and smiled. "This is your room, isn't it?"

She frowned and looked around at it. Nothing even remotely said it was her room. "Yes, but how did you know?"

"Smallest and the least nice."

She shrugged. "I never minded it."

"Of course you didn't." He walked toward her, and, on the way, he closed the door. "Come on. Get some rest."

"And you?" she asked, a bit of challenge in her voice.

"I'll lie beside you and make sure you don't have nightmares," he said firmly.

She stopped and stared. "How did you know I had nightmares?"

"I think we all have nightmares," he said gently. "For one reason or another. What you need is sleep."

She couldn't argue with that. She walked into the bathroom, scrubbed down as best she could, brushed her hair with a brush forgotten in one of the drawers and came back out again. "It'd be good if I had clothes."

"Everything's at Gunner's," Liam said with a chuckle.

She nodded, kicked off her boots, stripped down to her panties and bra, and slid under the covers. "Even if you were to try anything," she said, "I'd be too damn tired."

He chuckled. "You were the one kissing me earlier."

She yawned. "I was. But again we're back to *that I'm too damn tired.*" She closed her eyes and slept.

LIAM WATCHED AS she completely left behind all of today's events and drifted off to sleep without a care. It took special skill to do that. He hadn't mastered it himself. He walked to the bathroom and followed her ritual. He washed up as best he could, came back, stripped down to his boxers and crawled into bed beside her. He wrapped an arm around her and pulled her against him. She snuggled deeper into the curve of his body without a complaint. He kissed the side of her head and closed his eyes.

But he knew he wouldn't sleep. At least not like she was. Too much shit had gone on. Too many puzzle pieces remained adrift in his mind, and he needed to fit them all together. He would have to wait for some answers. But considering Brianna and Carlos had a deal with the mother to sell off a large portion of Jim's land to a big property development company and then to take the money and run, this was just the tip of the illegal-activities' iceberg.

He wasn't sure what the trio had planned to do with the elephants, if anything. Or if they would just keep sectioning off the land to sell to other people. He couldn't imagine them trying to kill the sanctuary because it did bring in

DALE MAYER

money. And it appeared they were very creative with accumulating money. He hoped the tax man had a really good look at Carlos's income. Liam would like to see all of them go to jail for a lifetime.

Lilianna had been through enough. With her father back in better health, Liam was sure she was happy to start fresh, finally not giving a damn about her sister, Carlos and her horrid mother—who Liam learned, via a text from the detective while Liam waited in Lilianna's room, were quick to turn on each other, each hoping to cut the first deal and get less jail time, less restitution. *No honor among thieves.*

As he lay here, his mind processing all the events, she murmured, "Stop thinking so loud."

He leaned forward and whispered, "I thought you were asleep."

"I was until I felt how damn good it was to be in your arms." She rolled over and stared at him, her arm sneaking up and around his neck. "And how much I really like being with you."

He dropped a kiss on her lips. "This is where we head into dangerous territory."

She smiled. "What's the matter? You scared? That's okay. I'll be gentle with you," she said with a chuckle. She gently stroked his bottom lip with her finger. And then she followed it with her lips.

He loved this playful side of her. This woman was totally content with her own sexuality, and that was damn sexy.

She kissed his lips, taking his lower lip in between her teeth and suckling it gently.

A pull deep in his groin had his body coming to life. He rolled over until he was stretched out on top of her. He kissed her gently at first and then with mounting passion as

224

she whimpered and moaned beneath him. He lifted his head and took a deep breath, trying to slow things down.

But she wasn't into slow. She grabbed him by his ears and tugged him closer.

He chuckled and said, "We have all night."

She shook her head. "No, we don't because, after this, I'll collapse from complete exhaustion," she murmured. "And then tomorrow the real world interferes again."

"But there's always tomorrow night," he whispered gently.

"Where are you living?"

"At Levi's compound."

She thought about that. "Not too very far away."

"Two hours from our side of Houston. So not very far away." Although privately he thought it was too damn far if this was what he would come home to every night.

"But it's not like a long-distance relationship where you and I live in different states," she murmured, kissing him gently and then deepening it, her tongue meeting his, coaxing him to slide past conscious thought.

He chuckled, but the laughter died on his lips as she pressed her pelvis hard against his. He shuddered, and she slid her hands down his back, stroking, scratching, caressing. When she reached his buttocks, she dug in her nails, and his hips responded, pounding against hers. She moaned, "Oh, yes." She whispered, "Oh, yes."

And he lost the little bit of control he'd had. He slid his hands under her bra strap, undoing the clip before tossing it to the floor, then pushing back the sheets so he could see the bounty before him. She lay on the bed, long and lean with full high breasts. He lowered his mouth, took in a nipple, tugging it deep into his mouth. She moaned and rolled beneath him, her hips moving, pulsing, her hands stroking, caressing, as she held him close.

He wanted to do so much more with all the heat throbbing through him, and he couldn't hold off too much longer. But he tried to make it last. Only she wasn't helping. She kept urging him on, her words driving deep inside him.

"I love what you're doing. Oh, my God! Yes, yes, yes."

His body was racked in shudders. He slipped his fingers inside the elastic waistband of her panties and paused for a moment, but her hips rose, her hand sliding over the top of his fingers, pushing him lower and lower. He removed the scrap of lace and slid his fingers through the soft moist area already waiting for him.

Gently he stroked her outside lips, then just inside the entrance to her body, her hips already pulsing, waiting for him to take her fully. She tugged at the elastic on his boxers and murmured, "You're wearing too much."

He slid a hand down, pulled off his boxers and settled himself between her legs.

Even then she reached between their bodies, her fingers wrapping around him gently, stroking, caressing him until Liam groaned. She wrapped her thighs around his hips and surged upward, seating herself where she wanted to be. He gasped, rising up on his arms, his head lowering as waves of heat rippled through him. She stroked his chest down to the curls at the apex of his legs and back up again, and then she wrapped her arms around his neck, and she started to move.

He groaned. "You'll finish this really fast," he gasped out.

"That's okay," she whispered. "It's all I can think about right now."

He eased onto her, his hands now grabbing her hips,

and, holding her firm, he took over. He drove deep and hard and fast, and then faster and faster. She came apart in his arms, her cries of joy filling the room as her body wrapped all around him. He wanted to take a moment to enjoy her reaction, to feel her own pulses as they wrapped around him. But he couldn't for long, and he drove deeper and deeper for his own end—finally reaching his climax as it broke over him.

She wrapped her arms around him tightly and held him close. Still connected as they were, she whispered against his shoulder, "If we stay like this, we could begin again in the morning."

He wanted to laugh, but the effort was more than he could handle. He didn't even get a chance to answer. She took a deep breath, let it out on a heavy sigh and fell sweetly asleep in his arms. He closed his eyes, held her close and thought about what a joy and a blessing she was in his life.

"My Lily," he muttered. Then he followed her into sleep.

Chapter 14

LILIANNA WOKE THE next morning to find Liam already hard against her. As soon as she opened her eyes, he whispered, "Thank God," and he plunged.

She went from zero to sixty instantly, almost shrieking with joy as her climax ripped through her moments later. She lay gasping on the bed. "What a hell of a way to wake up."

He kissed her hard. "And it's time to wake up. Your father will be here soon."

Her eyes opened wide, and she struggled to get out of the bed. She raced to the bathroom and hopped into the shower. He wished he could join her, but he could hear vehicles on the driveway. He dressed with a sigh and one last look at the bathroom and walked downstairs.

Logan was in the kitchen, pouring coffee. He looked up, a grin on his face. "You will treat her right, *right?*"

"Maybe the question is, will she treat me right?" Liam said with a wicked grin.

Logan laughed out loud and warned, "She's the marrying kind."

"I know. I've never met anyone like her," Liam said, a serious look on his face.

Harrison joined them in the kitchen, took one look at Liam's face and said, "Levi's luck holds. Who would have thought?"

Just then the front door opened, and they could hear Gunner and Jim walking in. Logan stepped into the hall and said, "There you two are. Took your sweet time, didn't you?"

Gunner walked into the kitchen. "Had to stop at the police station."

Lilianna joined them and poured coffee for her father and Gunner. She carried the coffee cups over. "And? What did you find?"

"Your mother is spitting mad," Jim said. "Apparently she and Carlos hatched the deal. Brianna went along with it because she was after the lifestyle and wanted to get away from the sanctuary."

"And yet Brianna always pretended to be so happy to be here," Lilianna said drily. "I wanted to look after the sanctuary, but Brianna made it very clear she didn't want me here."

"She had to be the one who handled the accounts so she could move money."

"Did she steal money from the sanctuary for her lifestyle? The penthouse?" Lilianna asked, her eyes narrowed on Gunner's face.

He nodded. "One hundred fifty thousand dollars' worth."

Her jaw dropped. "What? I didn't even know there was that kind of money here." She turned to look at her father.

He nodded. "I always kept more than $100,000 in a fund to make sure the animals had a couple years before we ended up in trouble."

Lilianna shook her head. "Oh, my God! I didn't even know."

"It's all right," Liam added. "A hell of a pile of money

was in that safe. We counted over $100,000 last night. That will go a long way to returning most of the embezzled sanctuary money."

"Well, that's something at least."

"It is now," Jim said.

The men nodded.

Gunner added, "As far as we're concerned, it belongs to the property because this is all sanctuary land."

"And my sister? What are the charges?"

"Fraud, for one. We'll have to wait and see."

Gunner nodded. "The lawyers are going through the accounting documentation right now, seeing how vast the damage is. But your father is back." Gunner looked at Jim who was leaning against the counter, his arms across his chest as he surveyed the land outside the window. "He might need you to stay with him for a while."

Lilianna's face lit up with love. "I really would like to. I need to reconnect with my father too." She put her coffee cup down and walked to him, wrapping her arms around him, and his arms opened up for a hug.

"I'll be fine," he said, "but, missing two years of my life, I could use some help to fill in a few gaps."

"Not a problem."

He looked over at Liam leaning against the counter on the other side of his daughter. "You're standing mighty close to my Lily."

Liam smiled at the "my Lily" reference, his arms crossed over his chest and nodded. "I am."

Lilianna tapped her father on the nose and said, "He's a good man, Dad."

He looked at her and narrowed his gaze. "He better be. No more men like Carlos will be allowed anywhere near you."

"That's fine with me," she said. "But no more Riannas either, right?"

Her father gave a mock shudder, hugged her hard and then released her. He poured himself another a cup of coffee, and said, "Damn, it feels good to be home."

She leaned over to Liam. He put an arm across her shoulders and tucked her up close, whispering in her ear, "Damn, it feels good to be home."

She wrapped her arms around him, letting her head rest against his heart. She knew exactly what he meant.

For the first time—maybe since forever—she felt at home.

Epilogue

NORTH DOCKTER WAS a sucker for a happy ending, which was good because Levi's compound was a bloody mess of sappy stories. With Liam having his very own Lily, he traveled back and forth to visit her at the elephant sanctuary when he had days off. Liam kept a room at Levi's compound, where Lilianna was a regular visitor here too.

Her father had stepped into his world as if he'd never stepped out. And it appeared the sanctuary was thriving under his leadership once again. Press releases picked up his miraculous return to good health, and the funds poured back in again. North was proud of everybody's contribution to that.

He was also particularly attached to one of the elephants: Billie. North spent more than a few hours a week visiting with her. Once Jim had roped North into giving Billie a bath—one of the best days of his life—he was hooked. He'd never been much of an animal person before, but Billie had changed that.

Now all North needed to do was find a life for himself. He wasn't sure how everyone kept coming up with partners. But they did.

Ice walked past just then. She stopped and looked at him. "You okay?"

He nodded. "How about you find me a partner too?"

She looked at him in surprise. "Of course. You're next. But I have to admit, most of the time the guys shy away from any involvement." Her smile widened. "They go into these kinds of jobs determined to not fall prey to the magic of love."

He shook his head. "Yeah, but that doesn't mean a whole lot. They end up completely in love by the end of one of their assignments. I'd like to believe in love at first sight, but it's something I've never experienced. Yet I did see it happening between Liam and Lily."

"Given the relationships that have sprung up around you, there's definitely enough evidence for you to believe in it. But I can't promise anything."

That made him chuckle. "Not expecting any promises."

"Good," she said gently. "Matter of fact, you're heading to England in two days."

He looked at her in surprise. "Why's that?"

"Charles Beckwith, a good friend and supporter in England, has a granddaughter in trouble. Her name is Nikki, and she's en route to his place. He couldn't get the full story out of her but said she was in tears on the phone. It's not minor, but he doesn't know how major it is. He's asked for our delicate touch to help her out."

North frowned. "What kind of problem?"

"No idea, but ..." Ice said sadly, "you'll be perfect for the job."

This concludes Book 15 of Heroes for Hire: Liam's Lily.

Read about North's Nikki: Heroes for Hire, Book 16

Heroes for Hire: North's Nikki (Book #16

In what circumstance wouldn't a knight want to rescue a damsel in distress? A former SEAL working for Legendary Securities, North Dockter has found the very circumstance that challenges even his stalwart, chivalrous ways. Nikki Beckwith is a firecracker who butts heads with him at every turn, refusing to follow orders or listen to his experience unless doing so suits her.

When she discovers someone is smuggling drugs through her company's warehouse and her life is threatened, Nikki flees to her aging grandfather's home in England to lay low and regroup. He's always been there for her, and, if ever she needed a bolthole to make changes in her life, it's now. Maybe it's time to return to the States…particularly after meeting North and realizing the attraction between them is more than she believed possible.

But Nikki soon realizes that no place is safe after her grandfather is attacked in his home. Even with her gorgeous guardian angel hovering close by, will she be too late to make all the changes she's envisioned?

Book 16 is available now!
To find out more visit Dale Mayer's website.
https://geni.us/DMnorthUniversal

Other Military Series by Dale Mayer

SEALs of Honor

Heroes for Hire

SEALs of Steel

The K9 Files

The Mavericks

Bullards Battle

Hathaway House

Terkel's Team

Ryland's Reach: Bullard's Battle (Book #1)

Welcome to a new stand-alone but interconnected series from Dale Mayer. This is Bullard's story—and that of his team's. All raw, rough, incredibly capable men who have one goal: to find out who was behind the attack on their leader, before the attacker, or attackers, return to finish the job.

Stay tuned for more nonstop action as the men narrow down their suspects … and find a way to let love back into their own empty lives.

His rescue from the ocean after a horrible plane explosion was his top priority, in any way, shape, or form. A small sailboat and a nurse to do the job was more than Ryland hoped for.

When Tabi somehow drags him and his buddy Garret onboard and surprisingly gets them to a naval ship close by, Ryland figures he'd used up all his luck and his friend's too. Sure enough, those who attacked the plane they were in weren't content to let him slowly die in the ocean. No. Surviving had made him a target all over again.

Tabi isn't expecting her sailing holiday to include the rescue of two badly injured men and then to end with the loss of her beloved sailboat. Her instincts save them, but now she finds it tough to let them go—even as more of Bullard's team members come to them—until it becomes apparent that not only are Bullard and his men still targets … but she is too.

B ULLARD CHECKED THAT the helicopter was loaded with their bags and that his men were ready to leave.

He walked back one more time, his gaze on Ice. She'd never looked happier, never looked more perfect. His heart ached, but he knew she remained a caring friend and always would be. He opened his arms; she ran into them, and he held her close, whispering, "The offer still stands."

She leaned back and smiled up at him. "Maybe if and when Levi's been gone for a long enough time for me to forget," she said in all seriousness.

"That's not happening. You two, now three, will live long and happy lives together," he said, smiling down at the woman knew to be the most beautiful, inside and out. She would never be his, but he always kept a little corner of his heart open and available, in case she wanted to surprise him and to slide inside.

And then he realized she'd already been a part of his heart all this time. That was a good ten to fifteen years by now. But she kept herself in the friend category, and he understood because she and Levi, partners and now parents, were perfect together.

Bullard reached out and shook Levi's hand. "It was a hell of a blast," he said. "When you guys do a big splash, you really do a *big* splash."

Ice laughed. "A few days at home sounds perfect for me now."

"It looks great," he said, his hands on his hips as he surveyed the people in the massive pool surrounded by the palm trees, all designed and decked out by Ice. Right beside all the war machines that he heartily approved of. He grinned at her. "When are you coming over to visit?" His gaze went to Levi, raising his eyebrows back at her. "You guys should come over for a week or two or three."

"It's not a bad idea," Levi said. "We could use a long holiday, just not yet."

"That sounds familiar." Bullard grinned. "Anyway, I'm off. We'll hit the airport and then pick up the plane and head home." He added, "As always, call if you need me."

Everybody raised a hand as he returned to the helicopter and his buddy who was flying him to the airport. Ice had volunteered to shuttle him there, but he hadn't wanted to take her away from her family or to prolong the goodbye. He hopped inside, waving at everybody as the helicopter lifted. Two of his men, Ryland and Garret, were in the back seats. They always traveled with him.

Bullard would pick up the rest of his men in Australia. He stared down at the compound as he flew overhead. He preferred his compound at home, but damn they'd done a nice job here.

With everybody on the ground screaming goodbye, Bullard sailed over Houston, heading toward the airport. His two men never said a word. They all knew how he felt about Ice. But not one of them would cross that line and say anything. At least not if they expected to still have jobs.

It was one thing to fall in love with another man's woman, but another thing to fall in love with a woman who was so unique, so different, and so absolutely perfect that you knew, just knew, there was no hope of finding anybody else like her. But she and Levi had been together way before Bullard had ever met her, which made it that much more heartbreaking.

Still, he'd turned and looked forward. He had a full roster of jobs himself to focus on when he got home. Part of him was tired of the life; another part of him couldn't wait to head out on the next adventure. He managed to run everything from his command centers in one or two of his locations. He'd spent a lot of time and effort at the second one and kept a full team at both locations, yet preferred to spend most of his time at the old one. It felt more like home to him, and he'd like to be there now, but still had many more days before that could happen.

The helicopter lowered to the tarmac, he stepped out, said his goodbyes and walked across to where his private plane waited. It was one of the things that he loved, being a pilot of both helicopters and airplanes, and owning both birds himself.

That again was another way he and Ice were part of the same team, of the same mind-set. He'd been looking for another woman like Ice for himself, but no such luck. Sure, lots were around for short-term relationships, but most of them couldn't handle his lifestyle or the violence of the world that he lived in. He understood that.

The ones who did had a hard edge to them that he found difficult to live with. Bullard appreciated everybody's being alert and aware, but if there wasn't some softness in the women, they seemed to turn cold all the way through.

As he boarded his small plane, Ryland and Garret following behind, Bullard called out in his loud voice, "Let's go, slow pokes. We've got a long flight ahead of us."

The men grinned, confident Bullard was teasing, as was his usual routine during their off-hours.

"Well, we're ready, not sure about you though ..." Ryland said, smirking.

"We're waiting on you this time," Garret added with a chuckle. "Good thing you're the boss."

Bullard grinned at his two right-hand men. "Isn't that the truth?" He dropped his bags at one of the guys' feet and said, "Stow all this stuff, will you? I want to get our flight path cleared and get the hell out of here."

They'd all enjoyed the break. He tried to get over once a year to visit Ice and Levi and same in reverse. But it was time to get back to business. He started up the engines, got confirmation from the tower. They were heading to Australia for this next job. He really wanted to go straight back to Africa, but it would be a while yet. They'd refuel in Honolulu.

Ryland came in and sat down in the copilot's spot, buckled in, then asked, "You ready?"

Bullard laughed. "When have you ever known me *not* to be ready?" At that, he taxied down the runway. Before long he was up in the air, at cruising level, and heading to Hawaii. "Gotta love these views from up here," Bullard said. "This place is magical."

"It is once you get up above all the smog," he said. "Why Australia again?"

"Remember how we were supposed to check out that newest compound in Australia that I've had my eye on? Besides the alpha team is coming off that ugly job in Sydney. We'll give them a day or two of R&R then head home."

"Right. We could have some equally ugly payback on that job."

Bullard shrugged. "That goes for most of our jobs. It's the life."

"And don't you have enough compounds to look after?"

"Yes I do, but that kid in me still looks to take over the world. Just remember that."

"Better you go home to Africa and look after your first two compounds," Ryland said.

"Maybe," Bullard admitted. "But it seems hard to not continue expanding."

"You need a partner," Ryland said abruptly. "That might ease the savage beast inside. Keep you home more."

"Well, the only one I like," he said, "is married to my best friend."

"I'm sorry about that," Ryland said quietly. "What a shit deal."

"No," Bullard said. "I came on the scene last. They were always meant to be together. Especially now they are a family."

"If you say so," Ryland said.

Bullard nodded. "Damn right, I say so."

And that set the tone for the next many hours. They landed in Hawaii, and while they fueled up everybody got off to stretch their legs by walking around outside a bit as this was a small private airstrip, not exactly full of hangars and tourists. Then they hopped back on board again for takeoff.

"I can fly," Ryland offered as they took off.

"We'll switch in a bit," Bullard said. "Surprisingly, I'm doing okay yet, but I'll let you take her down."

"Yeah, it's still a long flight," Ryland said studying the islands below. It was a stunning view of the area.

"I love the islands here. Sometimes I just wonder about the benefit of, you know, crashing into the sea, coming up on a deserted island, and finding the simple life again," Bullard said with a laugh.

"I hear you," Ryland said. "Every once in a while, I wonder the same."

Several hours later Ryland looked up and said abruptly, "We've made good time considering we've already passed Fiji."

Bullard yawned.

"Let's switch."

Bullard smiled, nodded, and said, "Fine. I'll hand it over to you."

Just then a funny noise came from the engine on the right side.

They looked at each other, and Ryland said, "Uh-oh. That's not good news."

Boom!

And the plane exploded.

Find Bullard's Battle (Book #1) here!

To find out more visit Dale Mayer's website.

https://geni.us/DMRylandUniversal

Damon's Deal: Terkel's Team (Book #1)

Welcome to a brand-new connected series of intrigue, betrayal, and ... murder, from the *USA Today* best-selling author Dale Mayer. A series with all the elements you've come to love, plus so much more... including psychics!

A betrayal from within has Terkel frantic to protect those he can, as his team falls one by one, from a murderous killer he helped create.

ICE POURED HERSELF a coffee and sat down at the compound's massive dining room table with the others. When her phone rang, she smiled at the number displayed. "Hey, Terk. How're you doing?" She put the call on Speakerphone.

"I'm okay," Terkel said, his voice distracted and tight.

"Terk?" Merk called from across the table. He got up and walked closer and sat across from Levi. "You don't sound too good, brother. What's up?"

"I'm fine," Terk said. "Or I will be. Right now, things are blown to shit."

"As in literally?" Merk asked.

"The entire group," Terk said, "they're all gone. I had a solid team of eight, and they're all gone."

"Dead?"

Several others stood to join them, gathered around Ice's phone. Levi stepped forward, his hand on Ice's shoulder. "Terk? Are they all dead?"

"No." Terk took a deep breath. "I'm not making sense. I'm sorry."

"Take it easy," Ice said, her voice calm and reassuring. "What do you mean, *they're all gone?*"

"All their abilities are gone," he said. "Something's happened to them. Somebody has deliberately removed whatever super senses they could utilize—or what we have been utilizing for the last ten years for the government." His tone was bitter. "When the US gov recently closed us down, they promised that our black ops department would never rise again, but I didn't expect them to attack us personally."

"What are you talking about?" Merk said in alarm, standing up now to stare at Ice's phone. "Are you in danger?"

"Maybe? I don't know," Terk said. "I need to find out exactly what the hell's going on."

"What can we do to help?" Ice asked.

Terk gave a broken laugh. "That's not why I'm calling. Well, it is, but it isn't."

Ice looked at Merk, who frowned, as he shook his head. Ice knew he and the others had heard Terk's stressed out tone and the completely confusing bits and pieces coming from his mouth. Ice said, "Terk, you're not making sense again. Take a breath and explain. Please. You're scaring me."

Terk took a long slow deep breath. "Tell Stone to open the gate," he said. "She's out there."

"Who's out there?" Levi asked, hopped up, looked outside, and shrugged.

"She's coming up the road now. You have to let her in."

"Who? Why?"

"*Because*," he said, "she's also harnessed with C-4."

"Jesus," Levi said, bolting to display the camera feeds to the big screen in the room. "Is it live?"

"It is, and she's been sent to you."

"Well, that's an interesting move," Ice said, her voice sharp, activating her comm to connect to Stone in the control room. "Who's after us?"

"I think it's rebels within the Iranian government. But it could be our own government. I don't know anymore," Terk snapped. "I also don't know how they got her so close to you. Or how they pinned your connection to me," he said. "I've been very careful."

"We can look after ourselves," Ice said immediately. "But who is this woman to you?"

"She's pregnant," he said, "so that adds to the intensity here."

"Understood. So who is the father? Is he connected somehow?"

There was silence on the other end.

Merk said, "Terk, talk to us."

"She's carrying my baby," Terk replied, his voice heavy.

Merk, his expression grim, looked at Ice, her face mirroring his shock. He asked, "How do you know her, Terk?"

"Brother, you don't understand," Terk said. "I've never met this woman before in my life." And, with that, the phone went dead.

Find Terkel's Team (Book #1) here!

To find out more visit Dale Mayer's website.

https://geni.us/DMTTDamonUniversal

Author's Note

Thank you for reading Liam's Lily: Heroes for Hire, Book 15! If you enjoyed the book, please take a moment and leave a short review.

Dear reader,

I love to hear from readers, and you can contact me at my website: www.dalemayer.com or at my Facebook author page. To be informed of new releases and special offers, sign up for my newsletter or follow me on BookBub. And if you are interested in joining Dale Mayer's Reader Group, here is the Facebook sign up page.
http://geni.us/DaleMayerFBGroup

Cheers,
Dale Mayer

About the Author

Dale Mayer is a *USA Today* best-selling author, best known for her SEALs military romances, her Psychic Visions series, and her Lovely Lethal Garden cozy series. Her contemporary romances are raw and full of passion and emotion (Broken But … Mending, Hathaway House series). Her thrillers will keep you guessing (Kate Morgan, By Death series), and her romantic comedies will keep you giggling (*It's a Dog's Life*, a stand-alone novella; and the Broken Protocols series, starring Charming Marvin, the cat).

Dale honors the stories that come to her—and some of them are crazy, break all the rules and cross multiple genres!

To go with her fiction, she also writes nonfiction in many different fields, with books available on résumé writing, companion gardening, and the US mortgage system. All her books are available in print and ebook format.

Connect with Dale Mayer Online

Dale's Website – www.dalemayer.com
Twitter – @DaleMayer
Facebook Page – geni.us/DaleMayerFBFanPage
Facebook Group – geni.us/DaleMayerFBGroup
BookBub – geni.us/DaleMayerBookbub
Instagram – geni.us/DaleMayerInstagram
Goodreads – geni.us/DaleMayerGoodreads
Newsletter – geni.us/DaleNews

Also by Dale Mayer

Published Adult Books:

Bullard's Battle
Ryland's Reach, Book 1
Cain's Cross, Book 2
Eton's Escape, Book 3
Garret's Gambit, Book 4
Kano's Keep, Book 5
Fallon's Flaw, Book 6
Quinn's Quest, Book 7
Bullard's Beauty, Book 8
Bullard's Best, Book 9

Terkel's Team
Damon's Deal, Book 1

Kate Morgan
Simon Says... Hide, Book 1

Hathaway House
Aaron, Book 1
Brock, Book 2
Cole, Book 3
Denton, Book 4

Elliot, Book 5

Finn, Book 6

Gregory, Book 7

Heath, Book 8

Iain, Book 9

Jaden, Book 10

Keith, Book 11

Lance, Book 12

Melissa, Book 13

Nash, Book 14

Owen, Book 15

Hathaway House, Books 1–3

Hathaway House, Books 4–6

Hathaway House, Books 7–9

The K9 Files

Ethan, Book 1

Pierce, Book 2

Zane, Book 3

Blaze, Book 4

Lucas, Book 5

Parker, Book 6

Carter, Book 7

Weston, Book 8

Greyson, Book 9

Rowan, Book 10

Caleb, Book 11

Kurt, Book 12

Tucker, Book 13

Psychic Vision Series

Tuesday's Child

Hide 'n Go Seek

Maddy's Floor

Garden of Sorrow

Knock Knock…

Rare Find

Eyes to the Soul

Now You See Her

Shattered

Into the Abyss

Seeds of Malice

Eye of the Falcon

Itsy-Bitsy Spider

Unmasked

Deep Beneath

From the Ashes

Stroke of Death

Ice Maiden

Snap, Crackle…

Psychic Visions Books 1–3

Psychic Visions Books 4–6

Psychic Visions Books 7–9

By Death Series

Touched by Death

Haunted by Death

Chilled by Death

By Death Books 1–3

Broken Protocols – Romantic Comedy Series

Cat's Meow

Cat's Pajamas

Cat's Cradle

Cat's Claus

Broken Protocols 1-4

Broken and... Mending

Skin

Scars

Scales (of Justice)

Broken but... Mending 1-3

Glory

Genesis

Tori

Celeste

Glory Trilogy

Biker Blues

Morgan: Biker Blues, Volume 1

Cash: Biker Blues, Volume 2

SEALs of Honor

Mason: SEALs of Honor, Book 1

Hawk: SEALs of Honor, Book 2

Dane: SEALs of Honor, Book 3

Swede: SEALs of Honor, Book 4

Shadow: SEALs of Honor, Book 5

Cooper: SEALs of Honor, Book 6

Heroes for Hire

Heroes for Hire, Books 10–12

Heroes for Hire, Books 13–15

SEALs of Steel

Badger: SEALs of Steel, Book 1

Erick: SEALs of Steel, Book 2

Cade: SEALs of Steel, Book 3

Talon: SEALs of Steel, Book 4

Laszlo: SEALs of Steel, Book 5

Geir: SEALs of Steel, Book 6

Jager: SEALs of Steel, Book 7

The Final Reveal: SEALs of Steel, Book 8

SEALs of Steel, Books 1–4

SEALs of Steel, Books 5–8

SEALs of Steel, Books 1–8

The Mavericks

Kerrick, Book 1

Griffin, Book 2

Jax, Book 3

Beau, Book 4

Asher, Book 5

Ryker, Book 6

Miles, Book 7

Nico, Book 8

Keane, Book 9

Lennox, Book 10

Gavin, Book 11

Shane, Book 12

Diesel, Book 13

Jerricho, Book 14

The Mavericks, Books 1–2

The Mavericks, Books 3–4

The Mavericks, Books 5–6

The Mavericks, Books 7–8

The Mavericks, Books 9–10

The Mavericks, Books 11–12

Collections

Dare to Be You...

Dare to Love...

Dare to be Strong...

RomanceX3

Standalone Novellas

It's a Dog's Life

Riana's Revenge

Second Chances

Published Young Adult Books:

Family Blood Ties Series

Vampire in Denial

Vampire in Distress

Vampire in Design

Vampire in Deceit

Vampire in Defiance

Vampire in Conflict

Vampire in Chaos

Vampire in Crisis

Vampire in Control

Vampire in Charge

Family Blood Ties Set 1–3

Family Blood Ties Set 1–5

Family Blood Ties Set 4–6

Family Blood Ties Set 7–9

Sian's Solution, A Family Blood Ties Series Prequel
    Novelette

Design series

Dangerous Designs

Deadly Designs

Darkest Designs

Design Series Trilogy

Standalone

In Cassie's Corner

Gem Stone (a Gemma Stone Mystery)

Time Thieves

Published Non-Fiction Books:

Career Essentials

Career Essentials: The Résumé

Career Essentials: The Cover Letter

Career Essentials: The Interview

Career Essentials: 3 in 1

www.ingramcontent.com/pod-product-compliance
Lightning Source LLC
Chambersburg PA
CBHW071508110726
47908CB00003B/762